The Mark of
Nimueh

www.**rbooks**.co.uk
www.**bbc**.co.uk/**merlin**

The Mark of Nimueh

Text by Jason Loborik

Based on the story by Julian Jones

BANTAM BOOKS

MERLIN: THE MARK OF NIMUEH
A BANTAM BOOK 978 0 553 82114 7

First published in Great Britain by Bantam,
an imprint of Random House Children's Books
- A Random House Group Company

This edition published 2009

1 3 5 7 9 10 8 6 4 2

The Random House Group Limited supports the Forest Stewardship Council
(FSC), the leading international forest certification organization. All our titles that
are printed on Greenpeace-approved FSC-certified paper carry the FSC logo.
Our paper procurement policy can be found at www.rbooks.co.uk/environment.

Mixed Sources
Product group from well-managed
forests and other controlled sources
www.fsc.org Cert no. TT-COC-2139
© 1996 Forest Stewardship Council

Typeset in 12/18 Bembo by Falcon Oast Graphic Art Ltd.

Bantam Books are published by Random House Children's Books,
61–63 Uxbridge Road, London W5 5SA

www.**kids**at**randomhouse**.co.uk
www.**rbooks**.co.uk

Addresses for companies within The Random House Group Limited can
be found at: www.randomhouse.co.uk/offices.htm

THE RANDOM HOUSE GROUP Limited Reg. No. 954009

A CIP catalogue record for this book is available from the British Library.

Printed in the UK by CPI Mackays, Chatham, ME5 8TD

*With grateful thanks to Johnny Capps,
Julian Murphy, Polly Buckle, Rachel Knight,
Sarah Dollard, Jamie Munro, Pindy O'Brien,
Filiz Tosun, Anna Nettle and Rebecca Morris*

Chapter One

It was a place no sane mortal would ever have dared enter. A freezing, airless cavern, buried deep inside the mountain, brimming with glistening stalactites which hung down like the teeth of some mythical monster.

And yet, in this lost chamber, someone stirred.

A young woman – alone in the icy blackness, her wide blue eyes surveying the vastness of the cave. The only movement came from the dancing flame of a torch as it cast ever-shifting patterns on the rock wall, its surface littered with primitive representations of ancient creatures. Entranced by the display, the woman contemplated the idea of these terrifying beasts living their lives once more, spreading fear and terror throughout the kingdom for all eternity.

She smiled.

All things were possible.

She glanced around the rest of the cave, but it was shrouded in darkness, nothing but the shadows to bear witness to her deeds. Satisfied she was completely alone, the woman positioned herself beside a large, circular basin made of stone, its weight supported by a plinth covered in intricate markings. She leaned over the bowl and gazed at her reflection in the pool of murky water. A beautiful, slender-faced woman stared back, her full red lips a stark contrast to her ghostly, pallid skin.

The woman plunged her hands into the basin, barely noticing the sting of ice-cold water as she bathed them. Then she picked up a small ball of moistened clay and turned it over in her hands, as if considering what to make of it.

She closed her eyes and concentrated hard, summoning the dormant forces that lay within her. Instantly an energy stirred somewhere deep inside and she felt it rise and swell throughout her body, growing more intense with each moment as it surged through her veins. She took control of the power and willed it to flow down through her arms to the very tips of her fingers.

Her eyes snapped open. Now she was ready to fashion the clay into a new shape.

A new *life*.

And then it surfaced at last, bobbing lightly up and down in a large pool of water. It was once again in a darkened underground chamber, but now many miles from where it had begun its journey. The egg floated on the water's surface, carried along to the pool's edge by the ripples of its own making. It came to rest and lay there in silence.

Suddenly there was a scratching noise from inside the shell. Timid at first, it grew ever more frenzied until part of the eggshell shattered, exposing a small hole. The creature poked a single claw through the gap, then with renewed vigour began to hack its way out.

Back in the cavern, the woman swept her hand over the basin of water and a shimmering image appeared. She smiled when she saw the remains of the egg – the jagged pieces of shell floating across the water's surface. She looked to the edge of the pool. The creature itself had already grown to twice its original size. Very soon, it could begin its work.

She moved her hand over the basin once more and another vision swam into view – that of a young man at a drinking fountain, gulping greedily at the water as it gushed from the tap.

The woman contemplated the image with a satisfied sneer. Her work was done and all was well, but she would have to be patient and let events take their course.

The waters in the basin began to swirl and bubble and the image shifted yet again. Her eyes grew wider as she saw the walls of an ancient city, its numerous gleaming towers soaring majestically into the hazy blue sky. She smiled balefully. It was a place she knew only too well, a city she would see destroyed at her leisure, its people brought to their knees in endless suffering and torment.

It was the city of Camelot.

Chapter Two

'Aren't you scared?' asked Merlin dubiously, keeping his distance as he watched Gaius work.

'Scared of what?' The physician turned to look at him.

'That you might catch whatever it is.'

Gaius turned his attention back to the corpse which was lying face down in the middle of the street. 'How am I supposed to find out what it is he died of if I don't even examine the poor fellow?' he said.

Merlin thought for a moment and shrugged. Gaius had a good point there.

The old man placed his hands under the cadaver, hefting it over. 'Anyway, I'm the court physician, Merlin. This is part of my job. Most of the time there's nothing really to be scared of . . .' He broke off, staring in silence at the ghastly sight before him, then looked at Merlin in open-mouthed horror.

Merlin met his gaze. 'You were saying . . . ?' He crept closer to get a better look. The dead man's face was unnaturally pale, the skin virtually translucent with a web of thick, blackened veins clearly visible underneath. Worst of all though were his eyes. They were fixed wide-open in a terrified stare, and a disgusting milky-white film covered the whole of each eyeball, the pupils and irises having all but disappeared.

Merlin had seen enough and he turned away, wishing he'd just stayed in bed. He'd been up since dawn, having been rudely awoken by a frantic, interminable banging on the door to Gaius' rooms. Their visitor was a man called Edmund, a petrified villager from the lower town, come to report the death of some poor soul who'd apparently passed away in the night. Gaius, in his wisdom and devotion to duty, had come running to see for himself. Unfortunately he'd insisted on Merlin coming too.

Merlin stood up straight and noticed one or two townsfolk milling about, looking in their general direction. The town was beginning to wake up.

'Um, Gaius, I think we might have a problem,' he said.

Gaius glanced around and nodded towards a piece of

sackcloth that was lying in the road. 'Quickly,' he said. 'People mustn't see this. They'll panic!'

Merlin grabbed the sheet and threw it over the corpse, covering its face just seconds before someone came walking past. 'So what do we do?' he said. 'We can't just leave him here.'

Gaius hauled himself up, his expression a picture of worry.

'Gaius?'

'We must get the body off the street and back to my chambers before people become too curious,' murmured the old man.

'But how do we get him back?' said Merlin.

Gaius arched an eyebrow. 'You'll have to find a cart or something. I'll stay here and guard the body. Off you go, and quickly!'

Merlin turned on his heel and ran off down the street, kicking up a billowing dust trail behind him. He sped past row upon row of tiny cottages until he came to a rickety house which leaned rather heavily to one side. A smile spread across Merlin's face. The cottage belonged to Tom the blacksmith, and there was a small handcart standing outside it. He trotted up to it and peered through the open window to see if anyone was at home.

He could see a young woman with black, tousled hair hurrying to and fro: Tom's daughter Gwen, a maidservant who Merlin had become good friends with soon after he'd first arrived in Camelot. She'd gladly help him. He was just about to knock on the door when he stopped himself, having second thoughts. Gwen would be curious to know why he wanted to borrow a cart so urgently first thing in the morning. In fact, knowing her, she'd probably want to come with him. He decided he'd better keep this simple.

With a sigh, he dashed off again, heading further into the lower town where the market traders were setting up their stalls. Thankfully he soon spied another empty cart, and set about haggling with its owner to let him borrow it. Five minutes later – and lighter by ten pieces of silver – he was thundering back up the hill to where Gaius was patiently waiting.

'Right, help me with the body,' said the physician.

Straining and huffing, the pair heaved the body onto the cart, taking care not to let the sackcloth fall off it. As they trundled the cart back down the hill, Merlin could have sworn they were getting strange looks from the townsfolk, and he kept glancing behind him to see if a stray foot or arm was poking out from underneath the cloth. He tried his best not to think of the grisly cargo they were carrying, but the image of those blank, staring eyes seemed to be burned into his brain.

Suddenly he noticed which street they were walking along, and he motioned to Gaius to take a small detour. He didn't want to walk past Gwen's house with a dead body.

At that moment, Gwen was still bustling about, making preparations for the day ahead. She rushed backwards and forwards in the tiny two-roomed cottage, stacking pots and tidying away clothes. Her father was pulling on his jacket, getting ready to go to work.

'Here's your sandwich!' she called cheerily, plonking a small package on the stout wooden table.

Tom grinned as he picked up the parcel. It was wrapped in brown paper and lovingly tied up with a neat pink bow. 'What's in it?' he asked, trying to sniff the sandwich through its wrapping.

'It's smoked pigeon,' replied Gwen. 'But I'd say there's more smoke than pigeon ...' she added mischievously.

Tom chuckled, stuffing the sandwich into his satchel. 'You're such a good girl to me, Gwen.'

Gwen smiled at him and snatched up a bunch of

tiny purple flowers from the table before heading for the door. She stopped and whirled back round again.

'Oh, I nearly forgot,' she said, 'I've done you some watercress soup for tonight.'

Deadpan, Tom looked at his daughter. 'Don't tell me . . . with more water in it than cress?'

Gwen laughed in mock horror and threw her arms round her father's shoulders, hugging him tightly. 'I'll see you later!' she said, and hurried out of the house.

Merlin heaved a sigh of relief as both he and Gaius hauled the handcart over the drawbridge that led into the palace courtyard. The body had nearly fallen off once or twice as they'd trundled over the odd pothole, but by some miracle, they'd managed to get back without anyone noticing it.

'Merlin!' came a cheery voice.

Merlin stopped dead in his tracks.

He whirled round and saw Gwen running up to him. This was all they needed. 'Oh, hi . . .' he said, setting the cart down. He hurried to the back of it, positioning himself between Gwen and the corpse.

'What're you doing?' asked Gwen, intrigued, trying to see what was on the cart.

'Ah, um . . . just moving something,' offered Merlin,

wincing inwardly. He turned to Gaius, but the physician simply smiled at Gwen and said nothing.

'It looks heavy,' said Gwen, peering at the lump underneath the sackcloth.

'It's nothing really,' said Merlin, sidling a little to the right and casually blocking Gwen's view once more. He racked his brains for a distraction, and noticed the posy in Gwen's grasp. 'Oh, someone got you flowers?'

'Oh, no,' she laughed. She smiled sweetly and Merlin looked at her. She had clear, light brown skin and kind, playful eyes.

'So, who are they for then?' he said.

'Oh, I picked them for Morgana,' replied Gwen breezily, referring to the beautiful young ward of King Uther himself. Gwen was Morgana's maidservant.

'I'm sure she'll love them.'

'Yes, well, she hasn't been sleeping properly,' said Gwen. 'I thought they might cheer her up.' She took one of the flowers and offered it to him. 'Would you like one, though? I've got plenty . . .'

Merlin took it. 'Thanks!'

'Purple suits you,' said Gwen brightly, then frowned as she noticed Merlin's red tunic. 'Not that I'm saying red *doesn't* suit you,' she said quickly.

He looked at the flower in his hand. Not quite

knowing what to do with it, he stuffed it into the top of his tunic.

Gaius coughed politely from behind him.

'Oh, well, better be getting on,' Merlin said, scuttling round to the front of the cart once more. 'See you later!' He smiled. Gwen waved at him cheerily and skipped on her way.

Merlin turned back and caught Gaius giving him a funny look. 'What?' said Merlin innocently. But Gaius turned away again and concentrated on pulling the cart the last few yards.

They finally made it to one of the side doors of the palace, and Gaius enlisted the help of two disgruntled guards to help them carry the body back to his chambers. Merlin was quite happy to let them get on with it. He'd done more than enough fetching and carrying for one day.

Once they were back inside, Gaius cleared some space on one of his workbenches so they could lay out the corpse. As the guards stomped out of the room, the physician whipped off the sackcloth and inspected the man's skin closely, his face alive with fascination. Merlin stared at the body in silence, wondering who the man was and who he'd left behind to mourn him.

'I've never seen anything like this before,' concluded Gaius as he finished his grim examination.

'Do you think it could be some kind of plague?'

'No, I fear something like this could never come from nature,' said the physician. 'But who has this kind of power?'

Merlin looked at him, registering the impact of his words. 'You think it's caused by *magic*?'

Chapter Three

There was a loud rap at the door and Merlin started as someone called his name.

'Answer it,' mouthed Gaius, and he moved in front of the table, blocking all view of the body.

Merlin obeyed and opened the door to reveal Arthur, the son of King Uther of Camelot. The prince's fine, chiselled features were set, his expression sombre. As Arthur's servant, Merlin could easily tell he wasn't in a good mood.

'Erm, I'm on my way. Sorry I'm late . . .' said Merlin, groping round for an excuse.

Arthur gave him a weary look. 'Don't worry, I'm getting used to it.' His eyes flicked downwards and his stern expression turned to one of puzzlement. 'What's that?'

'Oh,' said Merlin, realizing what he was looking at.

He snatched the tiny flower from the top of his tunic and twirled it around, slightly embarrassed. 'I met Gwen, and she . . . gave it to me.'

But Arthur had already lost interest. 'Tell Gaius my father wants to see him now,' he said. Without bothering to wait for a reply, he turned and strode off. Merlin watched his retreating figure with a sour look on his face.

He slammed the door shut, turning to his mentor. 'Gaius—'

'I heard,' Gaius interrupted.

'Why couldn't he just tell you himself?'

Gaius shrugged. 'Because that's the way it is, you're a servant.'

'If he knew who I was, what I've done for him . . .'

'You'd be a dead servant,' said Gaius curtly.

Merlin knew exactly what Gaius meant. Long ago, King Uther had banned all magic from the kingdom, and considered anyone who used it to be an evil sorcerer who deserved to be put to death immediately. For Merlin, this meant that he had to hide his own abilities – keep them completely secret from everyone – or risk execution himself. It was something he had to live with, every day, every moment. And it wasn't easy. Ironically Merlin had already secretly used his magical powers to save Arthur's life, and on the first occasion a grateful Uther had appointed him as the prince's manservant. It was a situation neither of the young men had been particularly happy about at the time.

'Right,' said Gaius, pointing to some sack cloth on another table. 'Fetch that and get this body covered up.'

'Hey, I'm not *your* servant,' said Merlin cheekily.

'No, you're my dogsbody,' shot back Gaius. 'Come on, hurry. We mustn't keep the king waiting.'

Merlin realized there was little point in arguing and did as he was told. With the corpse safely covered, the two of them hurried out of the room and down the small staircase that led to Gaius' quarters. Merlin questioned Gaius more about the disease and its causes as they sped along the palace corridors, but the old man's replies were vague and half-hearted. He clearly had a lot on his mind.

Minutes later, they reached the entrance to the council chamber. Two sentries were standing guard on either side of the great doors.

'I've been summoned to attend the king,' said Gaius importantly. 'Let us pass, please.'

Merlin eyed the two guards. They were holding

long, lethal-looking spears, and were dressed from head to foot in full battle armour, over which each wore a blood-red tabard emblazoned with the king's arms. They gave the briefest of nods, and swung open the heavy doors. Merlin followed Gaius into the huge, high-ceilinged room.

He gasped at the sight which greeted them.

There, sprawled awkwardly on the cold, stone floor, lay one of Uther's courtiers. Like the cadaver they'd discovered already, the man's skin was unnaturally pale, almost as if it had been bleached somehow. His eyes were fixed open in a manic stare, and the eyeballs themselves were completely white. On the floor next to the corpse lay a silver tray and two overturned goblets. The man had obviously been carrying them when he'd collapsed and died. Merlin's eyes followed the movement of the spilled wine as it seeped across the flagstone floor. It was a gruesome sight.

He glanced around the chamber, taking in the sea of distressed faces. The assembled nobles and courtiers were all frozen in terror, staring at the corpse in disbelief. Merlin's eyes settled on King Uther who was standing near the body, his strong, noble features tortured with anguish and concern. His son, Prince Arthur, was by his side.

Gaius bowed his head graciously. 'I came as quickly as I could, sire,' he murmured.

'What's happened to him?' asked Uther, urgency in his voice.

Gaius stooped down to examine the corpse. 'I don't know, sire,' he said after a few moments. 'This is the second case I've seen today.'

Uther's eyes narrowed. 'Why didn't you report it to me?'

'I was attempting to find the cause, sire,' said Gaius, straightening up once more.

'And what did you conclude?' pressed Uther.

'I don't think it's time to hurry to conclusions,' said Gaius. 'The scientific process is a long one . . .'

Merlin studied the king thoughtfully. There was something oddly unsettling about his manner. Outwardly he appeared calm, but to Merlin he seemed like a coiled spring, as if carefully suppressing his anger. Merlin knew that as a great warrior, Uther was used to being in complete control and hated it when explanations were beyond his reasoning.

The king moved closer to Gaius, searching the old man's face. 'What are you concealing from me?'

'Sire, I have seen nothing like it before,' said

Gaius helplessly. 'The appearance of the bodies suggests that this strikes them almost without warning.'

'What is the cause?'

Gaius paused, and Merlin glanced at him. He knew the effect the truth would have on the king.

'I think,' the physician said slowly, 'I'd have to say the cause . . . the most likely cause . . . is *sorcery* . . .'

Uther fixed Gaius with a steely glare and then pulled his son to one side, addressing him in a low voice. Merlin stepped forward to help Gaius with the body, his ears straining to overhear the king's words.

'You must find who did this,' Uther commanded softly.

'I will, Father,' said the prince.

'Conduct door-to-door searches,' Uther went on. 'Increase your presence in the town. Double the guards on all the gates. You must also lend the physician your servant.'

'*Merlin?*' exclaimed Arthur incredulously.

'We need Gaius to find a cure,' persisted Uther. 'He needs all the help we can give him. If Gaius is right about the cause, believe me, this entire city could be wiped out.'

'Wiped out?' Arthur looked at the king in horror.

'This is the kind of magic that undermines our

authority, challenges all we've done,' hissed Uther. 'If we cannot control this plague, people will turn to magic for a cure. The kingdom will descend into chaos and anarchy and we will have lost all hope.'

Arthur looked at his father and nodded grimly.

'We have to find the sorcerer and quickly,' added Uther. 'I want whoever is responsible for this evil to be found and executed before any more of my people die.'

'Yes, Father,' said the prince.

Uther gestured for Gaius and Merlin to take the body away. As Merlin struggled to lift the weight of the courtier, he watched Arthur stride out of the court, motioning his guards to follow him. His mind was reeling from what he'd overheard and he realized he'd been unconsciously holding his breath as he'd listened to Uther's doom-laden words.

Not for the first time, Merlin considered the precarious nature of his own position in the king's court, and he remembered the events that had led up to his appointment as Arthur's servant. He thought of his mother, how fearful she'd been that his magical gifts would one day be discovered in the tiny village where he'd grown up. She'd believed he'd be much better off under the wise and watchful gaze of Gaius, an old friend she trusted would guide and protect him and know how to nurture his extraordinary powers.

But as much as his new life in Camelot excited him, Merlin was beginning to wonder just how safe he really was. He'd already witnessed Uther execute a man for using magic and he shuddered, willing those terrifying memories to stay away from his thoughts. He watched now as the king paced around the hall, a look of grim determination etched on his face.

Merlin knew that Uther Pendragon would never give up – until the sorcerer was dead.

Chapter Four

Between them, Merlin and Gaius did their best to carry the body out of the council chamber, but it was so heavy, they quickly had to put it down again.

'I'm not used to all this exertion,' said Gaius, catching his breath. He beckoned to a couple of guards, and they came striding over to give them a hand.

They made their way back to Gaius' rooms in silence, and as they reached the top of the narrow flight of steps, Merlin pushed open the door, wondering where they'd find the space to put this second body.

To their horror, they found that in their brief absence, three more deaths had been reported. All the victims appeared to have suffered from the same terrible illness. A frightened servant was quaking by the door to the physician's chambers; he was clearly relieved that Gaius had returned.

'Tell me,' Gaius said urgently. 'What do you know of these poor victims?'

'Only what I was told, sir,' the servant mumbled. 'All have died this day – healthy yesterday, then falling ill and dying quickly.' He backed away. 'They say it is spreading fast . . .'

Merlin looked at Gaius in shock. Spreading! If they couldn't find a cure, how many more would die?

A grim look on his face, Gaius hurried about, relocating his precious equipment piece by piece. Impressively, even though everywhere else looked too cluttered already, he somehow managed to find room for all his bits and pieces. At last the guards set the body down on the table, then quickly marched out, slamming the door behind them.

'So what's next?' Merlin asked, a chill passing through him as he looked at the bodies. Gaius' room had turned into a morgue.

'I need to go to the market,' replied Gaius, snatching up a large wicker basket.

Merlin scrunched his face up. 'I don't think I could eat anything,' he said. 'I think I've lost my appetite.'

'I'm not talking about food, Merlin,' said Gaius. 'I need some more herbs, and besides that, I want to have a quick look around the lower town, see if there's any clue as to what's causing this disease. Come – your eyes may pick up some detail I might miss.'

As the pair left the palace, Merlin wrapped his coat tighter about himself, hugging it against the cold. They made for the lower town, but instead of finding the market bustling with activity, the whole area seemed strangely quiet. Merlin studied the faces of the townsfolk as they went about their business. They looked subdued, uneasy. Did they know of the bodies?

He tugged Gaius' sleeve as the old man bought some bunches of herbs from a stallholder. 'There's something strange in the air,' whispered Merlin. 'Can you feel it?'

Gaius pointed into the distance. 'I think that may have something to do with it,' he said. 'Arthur is acting quickly. See.'

Merlin looked up and saw Arthur and a group of guards talking to a man outside his house. The man looked scared, pointing wildly at the front door of his neighbour's cottage. A nod from Arthur gave his guards the signal to approach the door, which they duly kicked open. Arthur followed them inside.

Merlin was appalled. 'They can't do that,' he said angrily. 'I know who lives in that house.'

'Who?' said Gaius as a crowd of onlookers began

to gather round, babbling amongst themselves in hushed tones.

Merlin turned to him. 'It's a just a frail old woman who sells bread in the market,' he said. 'I've spoken to her loads of times. No way is she a sorceress!'

'I'm afraid where magic is concerned, Uther does what he likes,' said Gaius gloomily. 'No one in the kingdom is above suspicion.' He patted Merlin's arm. 'Let's go.'

As they moved away, Merlin could hear the sound of approaching footsteps. It had to be more of Uther's soldiers, their boots pounding the stony streets as they marched in unison. The platoon suddenly rounded a corner, heading straight towards them, each guard carrying a long, threatening spear. As they stomped along the street, the townsfolk quickly got out of their way, cowering in doorways.

'Come on, this way,' whispered Gaius, pulling at his arm, leading him into a quieter side street. As they hurried along it, Merlin noticed a man slumped by the roadside, leaning awkwardly against a wooden post. His clothes were ragged and dirty, his face turned away from them.

Merlin ran over to him, and as he drew closer he noticed how strangely pale the man's skin was. Merlin knelt by him, staring into his face. There was that same peculiar cloudiness in his eyes – even as Merlin studied him, the milkiness was spreading over his irises – and his features were twisted with pain as he fought for breath. He barely seemed able to focus on Merlin, but managed to lift up an arm, waving it about feebly.

'Gaius, he's still alive!' called Merlin, and the physician came hurrying over. Merlin lay a comforting hand on the man's shoulder. 'Can you speak?' he whispered. 'Tell us what happened to you.'

The man tried to reply, but the words seemed to die in his throat. All he could manage was a strained, rasping noise.

'He's delirious,' said Gaius.

The man's arm dropped down and his head fell to one side, his breathing shallower, as if exhausted by even this tiny amount of activity. 'Perhaps it's just as well,' said Merlin quietly. He stood up and looked at Gaius. 'He's still alive though, so you can try and cure him, can't you?'

Gaius shook his head sadly. 'I'm afraid it's just too late. There's nothing we can do for him. We don't even know what the disease is yet. All we can do is to try and make him comfortable – and hope that his suffering is not in vain, but that it helps us towards finding the cure.'

But as Gaius bent over the man, he realized that it truly was too late for this particular victim.

The man was dead.

'We have another body to take back now,' he said sadly. 'If only we could find a cure . . . But how?'

'With magic!' blurted out Merlin, shaken by the man's death.

Startled, Gaius looked all around him. Two guards had turned into the street and were busy questioning a young woman by the side of the road.

'Have a look,' whispered Gaius. 'They're suspicious of everyone! This is not the time to be using magic. Science will lead us to the source of the disease! We must go – now.'

By the time they got back to Gaius' chambers, Merlin was feeling tired while Gaius, in complete contrast, seemed full of energy. He started setting up an experiment, gathering together a cluster of small flasks and phials. Realizing there was little he could do to help, Merlin sloped off to his room, racking his brains for something positive to do – some way he could help to find the cure.

Then a thought flashed into his mind. He knew the very thing.

He lay down on his bed and reached an arm underneath it, pulling out a large leather-bound book. He sat up, holding it in both hands, feeling the weight of it. It was his most treasured possession, entrusted to him by Gaius.

It was a book of magic.

Gingerly Merlin began to leaf through the pages, marvelling at the hundreds of spells and incantations it contained, all written out in neat copperplate hand-writing and illustrated with scratchy drawings of all kinds of herbs and potions. He knew that by just looking at such a book, he was committing a terrible crime in the eyes of the king, but somehow that just added to the thrill of it.

As he began to search for the spell he needed, he noticed an acrid smell in the air – so strong it began to catch the back of his throat. He plonked the book on the floor next to his bed, then got up to open the door. He smiled as he watched Gaius at work, surrounded by flasks full of bubbling liquids, each giving off noxious fumes. The concoction of smells was almost overpowering.

'What are you doing?' he asked curiously, coming down the steps into the main room.

Gaius was heating up a small flask of milky liquid by

holding it in the flame of a candle. 'I'm examining the contents of one of the victims' stomachs,' he said without looking up.

Merlin pulled a face as he drew close. 'Will that tell you who did it?'

'No, but it might tell us how the disease is spread. One thing I do know is that this is magic of the darkest kind,' said Gaius gravely as he added a thick red liquid from another flask observed the reaction as the two substances mixed together.

'But I still don't understand why someone would use magic like that,' said Merlin.

'Magic corrupts,' replied Gaius matter-of-factly. 'People use it for their own ends.'

'But not all magic is bad. I know it isn't!'

Gaius shook his head. 'It's neither good nor bad. It's how you *use* it.'

Merlin was about to press him further when the door was suddenly thrown open. Three guards came barging in, Arthur following close behind.

'Over there,' Arthur directed the guards. Then added a little sheepishly, 'I'm sorry, Gaius, we're under orders to search every room in town.'

'What for?' demanded Gaius.

'The sorcerer,' replied Arthur. Regaining some of his

customary swagger, he nodded to his three guards, and Merlin stared in disbelief as they started raking around in Gaius' possessions. They searched under piles of books and peered into the dozens of stone jars which littered the workbenches. In fact, everything that wasn't fixed down was picked up and tossed aside, and it wasn't long before the room began to look even more of a jumble than usual.

Gaius watched them, his face full of fury. 'Why would a sorcerer be here?' he demanded.

'I'm just doing my job,' said Arthur.

'Well, we've nothing to hide,' snapped the old man. 'Go on then – search!'

Arthur sauntered over to a table in the far corner of the room and picked up a book from the top of a huge pile. It looked worn and dusty, the bindings all frayed at the edges. 'What are these books and papers?' he asked.

'My life's work,' said Gaius, 'dedicated to the pursuit and understanding of science. You're quite welcome to read through them, if you wish.'

Arthur instantly put the book back and it created a cloud of billowing dust as it thudded down onto the pile. He turned away, and pointed to the door at top of the short flight of steps. 'What's this room up here?'

'It's mine,' said Merlin quickly.

'What do you expect to find in there?' said Gaius, still rattled by Arthur's behaviour.

'I'm looking for material or evidence suggesting the use of enchantments,' said Arthur as he started to go up the steps.

Gaius drew closer to Merlin. 'What have you done with the book I gave you?' he whispered.

Merlin didn't answer. He could see the book of magic in his mind's eye, lying on the floor. Arthur would be sure to discover it at any moment, and Uther would have all the evidence he was looking for.

'Merlin, come here!' Suddenly Arthur's grave voice echoed through the open door.

'No,' breathed Merlin. He felt a lurching sensation in his stomach at Arthur's next words.

'Look what I've found . . . !'

Chapter Five

Merlin's heart raced as he leaped up the steps, his mind full of half-formed excuses, none of which sounded the least bit plausible. He entered his room with a sickening sense of dread.

To his astonishment, Arthur wasn't looking at the magic book at all. He was standing to one side, his back to the door. 'I've found a place where you can put things,' he said disapprovingly. 'It's called a cupboard!' He slammed the door shut and the rickety closet wobbled alarmingly.

Merlin let out a nervous laugh, unable to contain his relief. He watched Arthur pacing about the room, looking in disdain at Merlin's belongings which were scattered all over the dusty floor. Merlin glanced downwards and saw the book of magic lying in full view next to his bed.

Outwardly it didn't look remotely incriminating, but if Arthur should pick it up and glance at even a single page . . .

Luckily the prince moved to the other side of the room and proceeded to rummage around the items on a small table, picking up random books and papers and jumbled-up clothes, then discarding them as he completed his half-hearted search. His back would only be turned for a few seconds, but that was all the time Merlin needed.

He breathed in sharply, fixing his gaze on the crumpled, discarded tunic that was lying on his bed. He concentrated hard, and felt a familiar heat building behind his eyes as he summoned the energy from deep within himself.

Instantly Merlin's senses felt sharper, and he reached out with his mind towards the tunic. He could feel the texture of the material, even judge the weight of it. His eyes flashed, releasing the concentration of energy, and the tunic suddenly slipped off the bed, landing squarely on top of the book.

Merlin breathed easier, but he knew he wasn't out of danger yet. Muttering and tutting to himself, the prince had finished searching the clutter on the table and was now on his hands and knees looking under Merlin's bed, screwing up his nose in the process. Merlin tried not to laugh at such a weird sight – the great Arthur reduced to searching through his manservant's belongings.

The prince got up again, and with a last look around, went back down the steps into Gaius' room, Merlin following him to the door. He glanced back at the covered-up book and his eyes flashed brightly once more. Suddenly the heap on the floor moved sharply to one side and disappeared out of sight under the bed. Merlin sighed in relief. From now on he couldn't be too careful.

He went back down to Gaius' chamber and saw the old man standing there in stony silence. He arched an eyebrow, as if expecting some kind of apology from Arthur.

'How long do you think it may be before you find a cure?' said the prince.

'That depends on how many interruptions I get,' replied Gaius flatly.

'Of course, I'm sorry.' Arthur's manner softened a little. 'I'll make sure that no one disturbs you again. I realize how important your work is.' He turned to his guards. 'Come on, we're finished here.'

The men nodded. They seemed relieved not to have

to do any more searching in this chamber full of bodies and they quickly followed Arthur out of the room. Gaius shut the door firmly after them, then rounded on Merlin.

'You must keep that book hidden!' he said.

'No,' said Merlin quietly. 'We must use it now to uncover the sorcery.'

Gaius gawked at him. 'Don't be stupid!'

But Merlin was serious. 'If I have this gift, then what is it *for*?' he said. 'You keep telling me it's not for playing tricks!'

'You want to practise magic when the king is hunting for *sorcerers*?' said Gaius in disbelief. 'Are you *mad*? Merlin, your life is destined for more important things.'

'But if I don't practise, then how will I get to be this great warlock?'

'There will come a time when your skills will be recognized,' replied Gaius firmly.

Merlin shook his head. 'When? How long do I have to wait?'

Gaius stared at him. 'Patience is a virtue, Merlin.'

'What, sitting by and doing nothing – that's a virtue?'

'Your time will come,' said Gaius.

'Maybe I could have cured that man we saw!' said Merlin desperately.

'I know it's tempting to use the way you find easiest—' began Gaius.

'It *is* when it would save a life!' shot back Merlin.

Gaius was becoming more and more agitated, and he struggled to keep his voice down. 'It's no good just saving one person,' he said. 'We need to understand this illness, discover how it's spreading!'

'Arthur is out there right now looking for the sorcerer,' yelled Merlin.

Gaius shook his head in dismissal. 'A sorcerer who's powerful enough to do this will never be found by searching the town!'

Merlin looked away, fuming in silence. There didn't seem to be anything he could say that would convince Gaius his way was right. But he knew for certain that it was. It *had* to be. Whatever the risk to himself, it was his duty to save the lives of the people of Camelot. That much was clear in his mind.

He watched as Gaius fussed around his workbench once more, tutting to himself as he tried to find the various flasks and phials he'd been working with before Arthur and his men had turned the place over.

'Ah, here it is,' he murmured, his eyes lighting up as

he finally located the flask of stomach fluid underneath a pile of old papers. He held it up in the dim light and added a few drops of bright green liquid to it, squinting to observe the reaction.

'So what can we do – if I can't use magic?' Merlin murmured.

'The only thing we can do,' said Gaius, looking up at him. 'Hope that science can find the answer before the disease kills us all!'

The woman was pleased. Even as she stood alone in her cave of ice, she could sense that events were beginning to play out precisely as she'd predicted. The good people of Camelot had already started to succumb – there was nothing they could do to resist.

She passed a hand over the surface of the darkened pool in the stone basin and the magnificent city swam into view, its high walls and countless towers bathed in the amber glow of the early afternoon sun. A sneer spread across her face. How proud and mighty the place looked. How utterly indomitable.

'But, oh, how the mighty must fall . . .' she mused to herself.

A different image appeared. It was the great chamber beneath the city. She could see the large pool of water where her precious egg had come to rest. It was calm and still and she gazed at it expectantly.

Suddenly there was a tumultuous roar and a massive shape burst through the water's surface, sending waves sluicing over the sides of the pool. Slowly and deliberately a bulbous head rose up from the water, followed by a mighty torso and huge, muscular arms brandishing scythe-like claws. The creature's mouth opened wide and it let out an unearthly screech, the sound magnified a hundredfold in the vastness of the underground vault.

The woman threw back her head and laughed. Her creature was indeed serving her well. But it was still only the beginning. The beast screamed once more, submitting to the will of its creator, then it disappeared again, the waters swirling over its head.

Euphoric, the woman was impatient to see more. She flicked her hand over the basin and the image blurred and shifted again. The view this time was of the great palace square, but it was a sight she had never witnessed before. Usually it was teeming with citizens going about their daily business, but right now it was empty, save for rows of white bundles which lined the square.

She smiled. They were bodies of the dead, laid

out on the cold, grey flagstones, waiting to be committed to the earth. She could hear the Great Bell tolling mournfully in the background.

The woman watched as a young maid filled up an empty pail at one of the town's water pumps, oblivious to the contamination it contained. The woman regarded her with contempt. She could hardly believe how stupid these people were. They deserved to die.

And when the whole city was on its knees, she wanted its king – the great Uther Pendragon himself – to know who'd been responsible for its downfall.

Chapter Six

Arthur was exhausted. He'd been up most of the night searching the last few corners of the city with his men. All he wanted to do now was to catch a few precious hours of sleep, but there was something important he had to do first.

He needed to report back to the king.

As the prince approached the council chamber, he felt a mounting sense of apprehension, knowing how much his father hated receiving bad news. He nodded curtly to the guards at the entrance, and the great doors swung open. As Arthur crossed the threshold, his father came sweeping towards him, expectation in his eyes.

'We've searched everywhere, the entire city . . .' Arthur began.

Uther read his son's expression. 'And you've found nothing?'

'I don't know where else to look,' said the prince, shaking his head, wishing the excuse didn't sound so pathetic.

Uther began pacing about the room. 'Then I have no choice,' he said at last. 'I want you to impose a curfew. From tonight, no one is to be allowed on the streets after the Great Bell.'

Arthur nodded. 'Yes, Father.'

'And cordon off the lower town,' continued Uther.

'Why?'

'Because my advisors tell me that's where most of the victims are. Let's isolate it, stop this disease from spreading.'

Arthur frowned. 'What about the people who live there?'

'Don't you think I haven't considered it?' said Uther, a steeliness in his voice. 'But what else can I do? I have to protect the rest of the city.'

Arthur searched his father's face, registering the anguish and torment there. Doubtless he'd been agonizing all night over the best course of action to take, and clearly there were no easy decisions to be made. Arthur wished his own thoughts weren't so muddied by tiredness, then he might be able to suggest some other way.

He bowed his head and left the council chamber, forcing himself to banish all thoughts of sleep. He clearly had much to do.

Elsewhere in the palace, Merlin awoke with a jump. He could hear the sound of frantic banging on the door of Gaius' chambers, followed by the babble of hushed and concerned voices. He didn't need to go and look to see who it was – it was obviously someone else come to report yet another tragic death in the night. Memories of the dying man they'd met the day before came floating back to him. Death had occurred so rapidly . . . What if someone he knew were to become a victim?

The door slammed and Merlin heard Gaius shouting his name. He jumped out of bed, yanked on his clothes, then opened the door a little, just enough to peer through into the chamber beyond. Gaius was already busy, examining the body of the latest victim with fevered interest. Merlin breathed uneasily, thankful that at least the other corpses had been taken away for burial.

He crept into the room, staring at the latest cadaver on the table. Shafts of cold morning sunlight streaked through the windows, giving the victim's already deathly-white skin an almost ethereal glow. He peered at the face of the body in morbid fascination – blackened, spidery veins were visible through the translucent skin. He checked himself, suddenly feeling guilty at how he was becoming hardened to the sight of death.

He watched Gaius with interest. Yesterday, the old man had seemed weary and distant, but this morning there was something different about him. He seemed to buzz with a new energy, he even seemed excited. Merlin brightened a little. It gave him hope.

'Right, now let's see what we have here . . .' muttered Gaius. 'What's different about this victim?'

Merlin realized Gaius had switched into lecture mode. 'She's a woman,' he said. That was an easy one.

'Yes, I can see that,' said Gaius, pulling a face. 'You know, sometimes I do wonder whether your magical talents were given to the right person.'

Merlin bit his lip. He knew he'd have to try harder. 'Um . . . ah . . .' he stammered, looking for something clever to say. He noticed an ornate necklace hanging from the neck of the body. 'She's a courtier?' he offered.

'Ah!' Gaius gasped.

'But how does that help us?'

'Courtiers seldom go down to the lower town . . .'

Gaius raised his eyebrows expectantly, willing Merlin

to find the right answer. Merlin's mind went blank.

'So ... what does that tell us?' encouraged the physician.

'Er ...' Merlin screwed his nose up. 'That she hasn't spoken to any townspeople?'

Gaius winced. 'Yes ... it suggests that the disease is not spread by contact.'

Merlin suddenly felt the penny drop. 'And they probably eat different food!'

'Good!' Gaius beamed. 'Anything else?

Merlin racked his brains. 'I doubt they've breathed the same air ...'

'So what's the only thing they do share?'

Merlin felt the pressure, eager not to disappoint. 'Water?' he said tentatively. Gaius nodded vigorously, as if too excited even to speak. 'You think the disease is spread through *water*!'

Gaius heaved a huge sigh of relief. 'Merlin. You're a *prodigy*.'

Merlin perked up a little. He liked the sound of that.

Gaius reached underneath his bench and thrust a wooden pail into Merlin's grasp. 'Oh, I get it,' said Merlin with a snort. Prodigies were clearly still meant to fetch and carry.

He ran out of the palace, trying not to look at the ever-growing number of shrouded bodies lying in the square. As he crossed the drawbridge into the town, he slowed down a little, detecting a brooding sense of hopelessness in the air. Everyone he came across seemed worn down and troubled, with many looking like they'd barely slept. Merlin shuddered, wondering how many people had lost family or friends to the disease overnight. How quickly life could turn to death . . .

He stared at the ground as he walked past them, a churning sensation of frustration rising inside him. He'd been told so many times how special his gifts were, and yet here and now, as he walked the streets, he couldn't use his magic to help even one sick person.

He reached the fountain and began pumping the water, quickly filling his pail. He realized that all he could do for now was trust in Gaius. His mentor was old and wise, and now he'd found out how the disease was spreading, they'd surely find a cure in no time . . .

Suddenly a terrible shriek shattered the silence of the street. Merlin whirled round and was astonished to see Gwen running full pelt along the dusty road towards the palace, tears streaking down her face.

'*Gwen?*' Merlin yelled, but she seemed not to hear and hared straight past him, her red cloak billowing behind her. Merlin bounded off the steps, water sloshing out of the pail as he ran after her. He followed Gwen back to the palace, calling out her name, but it seemed like nothing would make her stop.

By the time he reached the steps to Gaius' rooms, Gwen had already burst through the door, her tearful voice drifting down the stairwell.

'Gaius, help me,' she sobbed, her words indistinct, punctuated by sobs.

'Gwen!' came Gaius' surprised voice. 'What on earth is it? You have the sickness?'

She shook her head. 'My father . . . his face . . . I tried to wake him up this morning, but he's so pale, hardly even breathing . . .' She broke down again, and Gaius laid a gentle hand on her shoulder to calm her.

Merlin entered the room and immediately saw Gwen's tear-stained face. He couldn't bear this. It was one thing not to be able to help a complete stranger, but this was a friend. A happy, loyal friend who'd never harmed anyone in her life. No way did she deserve this.

'Please, Gaius. He's all I have.' Gwen fought desperately to speak through her tears.

Gaius took her hand, great sadness in his eyes. 'Gwen, I have no cure,' he said softly.

'I'm *begging* you!'

'I wish there was something . . . anything . . . but so far the remedy is beyond what I can achieve,' said Gaius, shaking his head helplessly.

Gwen's face crumpled, her last hope shattered.

'I'm sorry, Gwen.'

Fighting back another torrent of tears, Gwen turned and sped from the room.

Merlin moved closer to Gaius. 'There must be something we can do,' he said determinedly.

Gaius took the pail from him and set it on his workbench. 'I'll do my best,' he said, collecting a sample of water in a small phial. 'Let's hope that this can provide some answers.'

'But that could be too late for Gwen's father!'

Gaius didn't look at him. 'I fear you may be right.'

Merlin's mind was suddenly full of ideas, a maelstrom of conflicting thoughts. Surely now was the time to act, to really make a difference. If this disease was caused by magic, then magic could cure it too.

As he stared at Gaius, lost in thought, he suddenly became aware of what the old man was doing. He'd picked up a small flower with tiny purple petals, and was turning it round by the stem. It looked oddly familiar and Merlin was sure he recognized it.

And then he remembered.

It was the flower that Gwen had given him. He must have dropped it. He noticed the fragile petals, some of them hanging limp where the flower had been squashed underfoot. Gaius stuffed the flower into the phial of water and squinted at it, as if waiting for some kind of reaction.

Merlin left him to it. He went up to his room and flung himself onto his rickety bed. He lay there, staring at the ceiling in silence, turning things over and over in his mind.

Slowly everything began to fall into place and Merlin finally came to a decision, a smile spreading over his face.

Gaius might not have any idea of how to help Gwen's father, but he did.

He had a plan.

Chapter Seven

The rest of the afternoon passed at an agonizingly slow pace, and by the time dusk fell, Merlin was going out of his mind with frustration. He paced up and down his room, desperate to put his scheme into action, but he forced himself to be patient.

He couldn't allow anything to go wrong now.

He went to the window and looked out onto the town below, the countless rows of tiny, ramshackle cottages, bunched so tightly together it looked like they'd actually been built on top of one another. One by one, tiny pinpricks of light illuminated the windows as numerous fires and torches were lit, banishing the cold and the darkness.

The sombre chimes of the Great Bell began to sound out across the city and Merlin searched for signs of movement, but there was no one to be seen apart from the occasional guard patrolling the perimeter of the lower town. With a shudder, Merlin remembered the words of a messenger who'd called on them earlier that day: '*The king has ordered the summary execution of any citizen who should dare break his curfew.*'

Well, Merlin had other ideas.

He forced himself to wait in silence just an hour or two more and he lay on his bed fully clothed, listening to the sound of Gaius shuffling around in the adjoining room, the chinking of glass tubes and flasks as he tidied up after himself. Merlin wondered absently why he bothered when the room was always a mass of clutter and disarray.

At long last, a faint snoring noise came drifting through the walls and Merlin got out of bed, then crept silently to the door. He opened it gently and peeped through the gap. Good; Gaius was already fast asleep, clearly exhausted from the day's hard work. Merlin stepped back into his room and closed the door as quietly as he could. The time had come.

He tiptoed across his room, wincing every time the floorboards creaked underfoot, like they were some-how conspiring to raise the alarm and give him away. Merlin knelt down by his bed, shifted a stack of books to one side and poked a finger through a small hole in the floor. He gave a sharp tug and one of the planks came free, exposing a small cubby-hole under the floor.

Merlin grinned. It was his secret hiding place.

He reached down and pulled out the book of magic, feeling its reassuring weight in his hands. He sat up on the edge of his bed and quickly began flicking through the pages, hardly daring to breathe, his palms clammy with sweat. This was surely the most dangerous thing he could possibly think of doing, disobeying the king's orders in such a flagrant manner.

Merlin rifled past the dozens of spells, all carefully recorded in florid, ancient script. Many of the pages contained references to obscure wild plants and herbs, most of which he'd never even heard of. After a few minutes he came across just the spell he wanted. Eagerly he read it silently to himself, repeating the words over and over in his head till he'd learned it off by heart. But that wasn't all he needed. Underneath the enchantment was a list of herbs and plants along with some scratchy, thumbnail drawings – ragwort, henbane, love-in-a-mist, fennel and sesame. He prayed Gaius kept all these dried herbs on his shelves.

He crept downstairs and began to rummage furtively around the jars and pots that spilled from the alcoves in the adjoining room. He kept glancing at Gaius nervously as he raked through his belongings, wondering how he'd explain himself if his mentor should suddenly wake up.

Merlin worked as quickly as he could, taking small amounts of each ingredient as he found it, making a pile of herbs in the middle of his handkerchief. When he was finished, he gathered up the edges of the material to make a pouch, then tied it up with a piece of string. He smiled to himself in the darkness, pleased with his progress. Then he began to think about what came next, and his smile faded. This had been the easy part.

With a last look at the snoring Gaius, he sneaked out of his chambers and down the staircase to the darkened corridor just beyond it. He paused, listening keenly for the slightest sound.

There was nothing. The whole palace was asleep.

He slipped out of the entrance, his eyes darting around the moonlit square. All was well so far, no guards anywhere in sight. Cautiously he made his way along the covered outer walkways of the square until he came to the great drawbridge. It was wide open. He was about to slip across it when he suddenly heard the stomping of heavy boots and a patrol came into view. Panicking,

Merlin pressed himself into a shallow alcove and held his breath, his heart beating loudly in his chest.

Unbelievably his luck held out. The guards clattered straight past him, and Merlin stood there panting, listening till the footsteps had completely faded away. Then he slipped from the alcove and ran into the night, heading for the lower town as fast as he dared and keeping to the shadows to avoid the patrols.

Soon, he came to the end of Gwen's street and began to move stealthily along it. There was no one about and he began to relax a little. Just moments later though, the sound of agitated voices came floating towards him. He stopped and ducked behind a cart, just as a patrol turned into the opposite end of the street. He peeped round the side of the cart. The guards were babbling amongst themselves, one using a pitchfork to stab at a large heap of hay by the side of the road.

Merlin shrank back into the shadows, frozen with fear, wondering for the first time whether he'd done the right thing. If he was caught the guards would kill him on the spot.

He peered round the corner again. The commander of the guards was now coming towards him. Merlin could make out a curious expression on his face, as if he'd been alerted by some movement and had come to investigate. Merlin ducked back again as the commander came nearer. Any minute now he would be spotted for sure and his luck would finally run out.

Then Merlin saw his chance, spying a barn door on the opposite side of the street, not properly locked by the look of it. He stared hard at it.

'*Onstyrian, onbregdan!*' He uttered the spell under his breath, and felt the familiar burning sensation behind his eyes as they flashed with an unearthly glow. The door suddenly creaked open and the soldier stopped in his tracks, twisting his head round to see what was there. Carefully drawing his sword, he edged towards the door.

Merlin screwed his face up in desperation. 'Come on, come on,' he breathed. 'Just a few more feet. You can do it!'

The guard commander seemingly obliged and stopped just inches away from the door, stooping down a little to peer into the gloominess beyond. Without warning, the door swung open sharply, smacking him in the head, and he crumpled to the ground, out cold.

Merlin heaved a sigh of relief, but there was no time to congratulate himself. Taking a quick look, and satisfied the coast was clear, he hurried along the street, stopping outside Gwen's cottage he peered through the window.

In the orange glow of the dying fire, he could see Gwen's father laid out on the bed at the far side of the room. His face was a mass of blackened veins, contrasting even in the half-light with the paleness of his skin. Gwen was slumped awkwardly against the bed, her head resting on her father's chest. She was fast asleep, her tear-stained face calm and serene. Merlin guessed she must have cried herself into a slumber as she'd nursed her ailing father.

With trepidation, Merlin tried the door. It was open; Gwen obviously hadn't had a chance to lock up for the night. Careful not to make the slightest sound, he inched his way forward. Unfortunately, he stepped on a loosened floorboard and it creaked loudly.

Merlin froze, wincing at the noise.

Gwen's face flickered with agitation as she stirred in her sleep, restlessly shifting about to find a more comfortable position. Merlin paused, praying she'd settle down again. Moments later, Gwen was thankfully still once more and Merlin crept forward again, taking the magic poultice from his coat pocket. He leaned over the bed and gingerly lifted the edge of Tom's pillow, planting the small bundle underneath it.

Merlin stepped back, fixing Tom with a wide stare. '*Pu fornimst adl fram guman!*' His eyes flashed, and suddenly a cloud of dancing flecks of light drifted from the pillow, enveloping Tom's head like a swarm of tiny fireflies. Then as quickly as it had appeared, the cloud vanished into thin air. Not taking his eyes off either of them, Merlin moved backwards to the open door before taking up position at the window, willing Tom to come round.

After what seemed like an age, his patience was rewarded. Tom slowly began to stir, and although the web of black veins was still clearly visible on his face, the deathly pallor of his skin had completely disappeared. With a groan, he instinctively reached out to his daughter, resting a hand on her sleeping head.

Gwen started, instantly awake, craning round to look at him. 'Father!' she gasped. 'What's happened? This is . . . I can't believe it!'

Merlin observed them in silence, grinning broadly as Gwen hugged her father, tears of joy and relief cascading down her face.

Then he slipped into the night once again, darting into the shadows whenever he came across another patrol. A feeling of euphoria had strengthened his resolve and he was soon back at the palace, having evaded the guards with relative ease.

Finally, still smiling, he slipped back into bed and fell fast asleep.

Next morning, the whole city of Camelot seemed aglow, its lofty towers shining like alabaster in the hazy morning sunlight. To many, the sight would have appeared impossibly beautiful, but its majesty and splendour was lost on the only person to witness the view. A young woman, entirely alone in her subterranean ice-cave, impatient to learn the outcome of her deeds.

She ran her pale, willowy hand through the chilled water in the stone basin and the vision of Camelot began to blur and swim before her eyes, the image that replaced it far more to her liking: a hundred or so shrouded bodies laid out in the palace square.

Things were indeed going well, but the woman was slightly disappointed all the same. She dearly wanted to see Uther's face, to learn of his plans and strategies for saving his dying kingdom. And then to revel in his despair. But she was sure she could wait just a little longer.

All that would come in good time.

Chapter Eight

Merlin was awoken by shafts of early-morning sunlight streaming in through his tiny bedroom window. He smiled to himself as he rubbed the sleep from his eyes. It was quite a pleasant way to wake up, and certainly made a nice change from someone trying to batter down Gaius' door. He lay in bed for a moment, pondering the events of the night before. Already they seemed hazy and distant, like some half-forgotten dream.

He got up, dressed quickly, then went down to Gaius' room, just in time to see the old man heading out. 'Where are you going?' asked Merlin curiously.

'I've no time now,' said Gaius. 'I need to see the king urgently.' And with that, he left the room.

Merlin couldn't believe his luck. With no one to

fetch and carry for, he had a few precious minutes of freedom. He pulled on his coat and dashed out, making for the residential wing of the palace. A few minutes later, he came to a grand staircase, almost knocking a couple of maidservants flying as he ran up it. He came to a stop outside the door to Morgana's chambers, trying to get his breath back. There was a familiar humming coming from inside the room, but no sound of voices.

Good. That meant Gwen was probably alone.

Merlin gingerly pushed open the door and saw Gwen hurrying about, busily sorting Morgana's clothes into neat little piles. He watched her in silence, relieved to see her happy and carefree once again, back to her old self. Merlin smiled. That had to mean her father was still all right.

Suddenly Gwen sensed his presence and looked up. 'Merlin!' she yelped, startled.

Merlin cringed. It can't have looked very good, spying on her like that. 'Um, hi,' he said.

'Hi,' said Gwen.

'How's your father? Is he feeling better now?'

Gwen looked taken aback for a moment, then she broke out into a broad grin, only too pleased to share her news. 'Yeah,' she laughed. 'It's incredible. It's a *miracle*! I still can't believe he's well again.'

'His skin's clear, back to normal?'

'Er . . . yes.'

Merlin beamed back at her, surprised the spell had been such a complete success. 'Well, that's great,' he nodded, and with a small wave of his hand he turned to leave.

'You don't seem surprised . . .'

His eyes flicked back to Gwen. She was looking at him strangely. 'No, I am,' he said quickly. 'It's a miracle. Got to be.'

The look of puzzlement grew on Gwen's face. 'But how did you know he was well?'

'Uh . . . because you're smiling.' Merlin shrugged.

'That's really weird. I haven't told anyone, but you know. How could you know?'

'Yeah, all right, you've finally found out . . .' said Merlin, taking a step towards her. I'll tell you . . .' He paused for dramatic effect. 'I'm psychic.'

Gwen smirked. 'No you're not!'

'It's true,' said Merlin, deadpan. He was enjoying this.

'All right, what am I thinking?' said Gwen, playing along.

Merlin's eyes narrowed. 'That I'm *not* psychic?'

Gwen erupted into laughter, shaking her head.

'You're *strange!*' Merlin frowned. 'Oh, I don't mean that in a nasty way,' she added hastily. 'You're just . . . *funny*. I like that.'

Merlin smiled. 'Well, I'm pleased for you,' he said.

'Thank you.'

'What for?'

She shook her head. 'I don't know, just for asking.'

'I didn't like seeing you upset.' There was a pause. 'Um, I have to get on,' he said, and with a last wave to Gwen, he hurried out of the room.

Meanwhile, after waiting some time for Uther to arrive at the council chamber, Gaius was finally in an emergency meeting with both the king and Prince Arthur. A drawn and beleaguered Uther, desperate for some positive development, regarded the object Gaius had brought before him with bemusement. 'A flower?' he said irritably. 'What is this, Gaius?'

'This is no ordinary flower, sire,' explained the physician, gesturing to the small phial on the table in front of him. 'I believe it holds the key to the disease.'

Arthur went to pick it up, but Gaius raised his hand sharply. 'Don't touch it,' he warned.

'What have you learned from it, Gaius?' said Uther.

'Sire, this flower is not naturally white. It was vivid purple when I put it in the water, and it's only been there a matter of hours.'

Uther stared at the bleached flower. 'And where's the water from?'

'The pump where the people take their daily supply.'

Arthur was alarmed. 'Then we have to stop them from using it!'

Gaius peered at him over the top of his spectacles. 'This city cannot survive without water,' he said flatly.

'We have to find this sorcerer . . .' stormed Uther as he began to pace the room.

'I don't believe he is anywhere in Camelot,' reasoned Arthur. 'I've been over the entire city, there's nowhere left for anyone to hide.'

'Then extend the search to the villages.'

'We've started, Father,' said the prince, 'but I can't search the entire kingdom.'

Uther glared at him. 'And I can't stand by and watch our people dying!'

Arthur decided there was no point arguing any more. Without another word, he bowed and left the chamber to carry out his father's wishes. He summoned his guard commander, Gregory, and gave him new orders to have the city guards redouble their efforts. He also sent out mounted messengers to ride swiftly to Uther's most loyal and trusted knights, commanding them to employ their own men-at-arms to join in the search for the sorcerer.

But even with that all done, Arthur was left with nagging doubts. 'Is there nothing more we can do?' he said as he strode through the town with Gregory. 'There must be something we haven't thought of . . .'

'We're searching all we can, sire,' said his commander, 'but I'm afraid some of our own guards have succumbed to the disease. The task only grows harder.'

Arthur nodded grimly.

'There is something, though . . .' began Gregory.

'What is it?'

'You commanded us to report anything unusual or strange . . .' Gregory pointed down the street. Arthur looked and saw Gwen's father hard at work, beating a piece of metal into shape with gusto.

'The blacksmith?' said Arthur. 'What about him?'

'One of my men told me he had the white death only yesterday,' explained Gregory. 'He was so frail with the plague that his neighbours believed he wouldn't see out the night.'

'That's interesting,' mused Arthur. 'Why should the blacksmith be so special?' He pushed his way through the gathering crowd of onlookers and went marching up to Tom. 'The story is you were sick,' he said bluntly. It sounded more like an accusation than a question.

Tom nodded his head respectfully. 'Not any more, sire,' he beamed, the prince's suspicion completely lost on him.

Arthur's eyes narrowed. 'Perhaps you were suffering from some other ailment?'

Tom shook his head. 'You're joking. I felt like death itself. Not enough strength in me to stir the air!'

'Then what happened?'

'I don't know,' shrugged Tom. 'Suddenly it was gone. And I'm fitter now than I was before.'

'That's remarkable . . .' Arthur's face clouded. There was something about the blacksmith's story that didn't ring true. 'Was there anybody with you when all this happened?'

'Just my daughter, Gwen,' said Tom, now somewhat perturbed himself. This wasn't the reaction he was expecting. While his neighbours had been astonished to see him recover, they'd been undeniably happy for him as well.

Arthur said nothing more. He turned on his heel and marched away, his men following close behind.

'What do you think, sire?' asked Gregory, trying to read Arthur's impassive expression. 'What do you make of his story?'

'I won't know what to think till we've searched the blacksmith's house . . .' replied Arthur. 'Lead me to it.'

Arthur swept through the streets with his entourage of guards and soon came across the tiny ramshackle cottage shared by Tom and his daughter. With a curt nod to Gregory, he stepped aside and two of the guards burst through the door.

'Search for anything at all you believe to be suspicious and show it to me at once,' ordered Arthur.

The guards obeyed and quickly began rifling through Tom and Gwen's meagre belongings. Arthur observed them in stony silence.

It didn't take them long to find what they were looking for.

One of the guards searching Tom's lumpy bed lifted up the pillows. Immediately an ethereal incandescence spilled out into the room, bathing the rough grey walls in a golden glow. Even though it had done its work, the healing rays of Merlin's poultice had refused to die down.

Gregory turned to Arthur, elated at the discovery. 'We've found our sorcerer, sire!' he exclaimed.

Arthur nodded. 'It would seem so. Conceal it and bring it with us. If she isn't here, then she's likely to be at the palace.'

'You mean Morgana's maidservant, Gwen?' said Gregory.

'Yes . . .' said Arthur uncertainly. He knew this was going to be far from easy.

Flanked by his guards, he headed swiftly back to the palace, making straight for Morgana's chambers. As he barged through the door, he mercifully found Gwen all alone, carefully arranging a bunch of wild flowers in a vase. She looked up in surprise at the intrusion.

'Seize her!' ordered Arthur, and the guards grabbed Gwen's arms roughly.

'No!' screamed Gwen, losing her grip on the vase. It fell to the ground, the delicate flowers instantly pulverized under the boots of Arthur's men as they struggled to arrest her.

'Guinevere,' began Arthur, 'I'm arresting you for crimes in contravention to the laws of Camelot, that you did practise enchantments . . .'

Just then, a woman came bursting into the room, her long, flowing robes billowing around her.

It was Morgana.

'Gwen!' she yelled, taking in the chaotic scene before her.

By now, the guards had almost bundled Gwen out of the room, but she managed to twist her head round, her face contorted in terror. 'What have I done?' she cried. 'I haven't done anything!' But the guards were too strong for her and proceeded to drag her out into the corridor. 'Help me, please!' she screamed.

Morgana rounded on Arthur, her wide eyes blazing with fury. 'What are you doing?' she shouted.

'I found a magic poultice in her house,' he said, avoiding her glare.

'That's ridiculous!' spat Morgana.

'How else do you explain her father's miraculous recovery?'

'Well, she's innocent,' retorted Morgana. 'I *know* she's innocent.'

Arthur shook his head. He'd known this was going to be hard, but it was even worse than he'd feared. 'What can I do?' he said. 'I can't turn a blind eye.' Morgana gave him a last venomous look and made for the door. 'Where are you going?' Arthur called after her.

Morgana turned round, her expression grim. 'To talk to Uther myself and put a stop to this madness,' she said determinedly. 'Gwen might not be able to convince him she's innocent. But I will.'

Chapter Nine

'Where are we going?' Merlin asked Gaius as they hurried along the palace corridors.

'To see an old friend,' replied Gaius absently. 'I need to find out about the city's water supply and I'm hoping he'll be able to help us.'

They turned a corner and Merlin noticed they were in a part of the palace he barely recognized. Minutes later, they came to a small, unassuming door at the end of a long corridor. Gaius knocked on it.

'Come in!' came a voice from inside.

Gaius opened the door, and Merlin found himself in a large gloomy room stacked with row upon row of dusty old books and rolls of parchment. Shafts of sunlight streaked through the stained-glass window at the far end of the room, illuminating the clouds of dust particles which hung in the musty air. Below the window was a large desk, behind which sat an old man, scribbling away intently with his quill and parchment. He had a bald head and bushy white beard, and his burly frame was swathed in fine brown robes.

They moved closer, but the man seemed to have forgotten all about them and carried on writing.

'Geoffrey?' said Gaius warmly.

The old man looked up suddenly. 'Gaius!' He smiled amiably. 'How are you? I hear you've been working hard to thwart this terrible disease.'

'Indeed,' nodded Gaius solemnly. 'In fact, that's why I'm here. I need your assistance.'

Feeling somewhat ignored, Merlin coughed, and the two men turned to look at him. 'Oh, this is Merlin,' said Gaius. 'A young scholar who has been placed in my charge.'

'Oh, has he really?' said Geoffrey, giving Merlin a disapproving look.

'And this is Geoffrey of Monmouth,' Gaius continued. 'Keeper of the Hall of Records.'

'What can I do to help?' offered Geoffrey.

'We've learned that the water's been contaminated with the plague,' said Gaius. 'I need to know how that could happen.'

Geoffrey frowned. 'You'll need to see the plans of

Camelot then,' he said thoughtfully. 'But I'm not sure the drawings of the water system exist any more. Many old documents were destroyed by fire some years ago.'

Gaius looked at him seriously. 'I've a feeling it could be very important, Geoffrey. Could you at least try and find them for us?'

His old friend looked uncertain for a moment, then broke out into a determined smile. 'Leave it with me and I shall do my best!'

Gaius thanked him warmly and nodded to Merlin. They left Geoffrey to his work. As they made their way back to Gaius' rooms, Merlin was sure he could hear the sound of shouting in the distance.

'What's that? Can you hear it?' he said.

As the two of them hurried along, the yells became louder and louder. Merlin blanched, recognizing one of the voices. It was Gwen's. He started to run, and as he rounded a corner, he was just in time to see Gwen being half carried, half dragged along the corridor by two guards, Arthur several paces ahead of the party. Merlin watched, dumb-struck, as she shouted and struggled, protesting her innocence over and over again. 'Let me go, please!' she wailed. 'I haven't done anything, I swear . . . ' But her pleas went unheeded as the guards dragged her forcibly towards the council chamber.

Merlin felt a cold stab of fear as it dawned on him what was happening. There was only one reason why Gwen would have been arrested. Arthur must have found the poultice in her cottage. He watched helplessly as Gwen twisted her head round. He saw the terror on her tear-stained face. 'Merlin!' she screamed. 'Merlin, please help me!'

He was about to run after her when he felt a vice-like grip on his arm, and the next thing he knew he was back in Gaius' rooms. The door slammed shut and the glowering face of the physician suddenly filled his vision. 'What have you *done?*' bawled the old man.

'What?' said Merlin, startled.

'I warned you!' said Gaius, glaring at Merlin so fiercely it felt like his stare was boring right through into his brain. 'I suppose you're going to tell me you thought you were doing the right thing!' Gaius stormed.

'I couldn't let her father die, knowing I could cure him,' protested Merlin.

Gaius looked at him in disbelief. 'Did you not think it might look a bit suspicious? The curing of *one man?*'

'Then all I have to do is . . .' Merlin began, his mind a tumult of rage and confusion. 'I'll . . . cure everyone! No one will ever have to know it was magic.'

'It's too late,' scoffed Gaius. 'They believe Gwen's the sorceress. They think she caused the disease!'

'I have to do something!' Merlin's heart raced as he tried desperately to think of a solution. He grabbed the door handle. He had to get out of the room, if only to escape Gaius' tirade for a few minutes.

'And how are you going to prove she's innocent?'

Merlin gave him one last look, but said nothing. He slammed the door and hared through the palace, making for the council chamber. As he raced along, vivid memories crowded his thoughts, a terrifying blur of chaotic images and sounds. There was one memory in particular that had seared itself onto his mind, a memory so raw and horrific it refused to disappear, no matter how much he willed it to.

The image of an axe flashed into his mind, held aloft by unseen hands, the blade glinting malevolently in the harsh sunlight. He saw the king's face, cold and dispassionate, casting judgement on the sorcerer. Yet again, he could feel the charged emotion of the crowd as they heaved and pushed, their revulsion and horror as the axe fell.

The terrible, sickening sound of a life cut short.

And then he thought of Gwen. Harmless, well-meaning Gwen. A girl so full of joy and happiness, who'd barely spoken in anger or hurt anyone in her whole life. Now she was about to share the same fate as that poor man.

And it was all Merlin's fault.

Overcome by waves of guilt, he ran faster, reaching the doors of the council chamber just in time to see Gwen being brought before the king.

'Please believe me, I've done nothing,' she whimpered, trying in vain to attract the attention of her two guards. 'I swear I haven't done any—'

She broke off as the soldiers shoved her sharply to the floor. She landed awkwardly on the cold marble, letting out a gasp of pain. Merlin glared at the guards as they took a step back.

With all eyes on the suspected sorceress, Merlin took the opportunity to slip through the open doors, hiding behind a curtain at the back of the chamber. He scanned the scene before him. The room was teeming with stony-faced courtiers and nobles, all staring at Gwen with mistrust and suspicion. It was as if they'd already made up their minds about her guilt.

The king himself was seated on his throne at the far end of the hall, his face unreadable as he stared at the woman on the floor before him. He turned imperiously to address Arthur, who was standing to one side of Gwen.

'Well done,' he murmured. Arthur looked uneasy, barely acknowledging his father's praise.

'Why will no one believe me?' wept Gwen, looking about her timidly, appealing to the mass of mistrustful faces. As her eyes swept past Merlin, he turned away in case she saw him.

And he hated himself for it.

'He got better, he just recovered. I didn't do anything!' Gwen's voice began to crack, the enormity of the accusation finally sinking in.

'I believe you!' Another woman's voice echoed round the hall, strong and confident. From behind the crowd, Merlin craned his neck to see who it was. Morgana stepped forward to confront the king, a dazzling presence in her purple robes. 'Perhaps this is a disease that is not always fatal. Have you thought of that? Perhaps he recovered naturally.'

There was a long pause and Morgana's words seemed to hang in the air. Merlin hoped she might have planted a seed of doubt in Uther's mind, enough to at least make him show leniency. Merlin stared at him expectantly, but he appeared unconvinced.

'Then what of this poultice that was found?' he said.

Morgana had no answer. She glanced down at Gwen

who shifted about on the floor in confusion. 'What poultice?' she said, wide-eyed. 'I don't know anything about a poultice.'

Arthur produced the glowing object from his coat pocket, and the gathered onlookers reacted to its unearthly shimmer with muted gasps of horror.

Merlin couldn't bear to look at it. He was such an idiot – he hadn't even thought to retrieve the poultice, let alone considered the consequences of its potential discovery.

'This was found in your house!' said Uther menacingly.

'I swear, sire,' protested Gwen, shaking her head vigorously, 'I have never seen that poultice before.'

Uther rose up from his throne, towering above her. 'Undo this enchantment,' he commanded. 'Put an end to this contagion!'

Gwen shook her head again. 'I can't!' she whimpered. 'I don't know how to.'

'Then I can show you no mercy,' said Uther gravely.

'But I am not a witch, sire,' pleaded Gwen. 'I don't know how to stop the illness.'

'If you will not undo your sorcery, then you force my hand and I must find you guilty.'

'I've told you I'm—'

Uther cut her off. 'It is therefore my duty to pronounce judgement . . .' he said, bearing down on her. 'And under the circumstances, I have no choice but to sentence you to death.'

Merlin's blood ran cold and he closed his eyes. This couldn't be happening. He wanted to blot out everything – Uther, Camelot, the entire world. He was dimly aware of Gwen's terrified pleas, begging Uther to listen to her, then the king's harsh tones as he silenced her. 'I can only hope that when you die, this evil plague dies with you,' he spat.

'No! *No!*' Gwen's piercing screams went right through Merlin as the guards snatched her up from the floor and heaved her out of the room. 'Please, help me! Please, I beg you!'

Broken and desolate, Merlin followed in her wake, not knowing who to turn to. The courtiers all took their leave of the king and jostled past Merlin as they filed down the corridor. He felt so numb, he barely noticed anyone around him.

But maybe there was just one glimmer of hope for him to cling to.

With Uther still to pronounce the exact time of Gwen's execution, he might have time to put things right and save her. He didn't know whether he had days, or just a few scant hours, but it was something he had to do. Otherwise he knew he would never be able to live with himself.

With the onlookers finally dispersed, Uther was left alone with Arthur and Morgana, his ward staring at him in horrified disbelief. He avoided her gaze and walked over to a table against the far wall and began pouring himself a generous goblet of wine. Arthur watched them both expectantly.

'I know Gwen,' began Morgana, attempting to make her guardian see reason. 'She's my maidservant, not an enchantress.'

Uther turned sharply, fixing his eyes on Morgana. 'Have you ever *seen* an enchantress?' he asked coldly. 'Believe me, they bear no sign, no mark . . . there is no sense of evil in the eye.'

Morgana shook her head defiantly. 'All of that may be true, but it doesn't prove Gwen is one. I've seen with my own eyes the way that girl works. Her fingers are worn, her nails are broken. If she was a sorceress, why would she do this?' Uther ignored her, taking a sip of wine. 'Why would she kneel on a cold stone floor, morning after morning, when she could make these things happen with the snap of her fingers' — she paused, choosing her next words carefully — 'like an idle king.'

Uther turned on her, his eyes flashing. 'You have no right!'

'But you have the right to judge over this poor girl's life!' retaliated Morgana.

'I have a responsibility to take care of this kingdom!' bawled Uther. 'I take no pleasure in this!'

'You're sentencing the wrong person!' persisted Morgana.

'She's right, Father.' Morgana turned round in surprise as Arthur stepped forward. 'You hear the word magic, and you no longer listen.'

'And have you forgotten what you yourself discovered in her house?' glared Uther. 'You saw evidence she had used enchantments.'

'Yes, maybe . . .' said Arthur, caught off-guard. 'But that was to save her dying father. That doesn't make her guilty of creating a plague. One's the act of kindness, of love — the other, of evil. I don't believe evil is in this girl's heart.'

Uther remained unbowed. 'I have witnessed what witchcraft can do,' he murmured. 'I have suffered at its hand. I cannot take that chance. If there is the slightest doubt about this girl, she must die or the whole kingdom may perish.'

'I understand that,' said Arthur.

His father looked at him. 'One day, you may become king,' he said. 'Then you will understand that such decisions *must* be made. There are dark forces that threaten this kingdom.'

'I know. Witchcraft is an evil, Father,' said Arthur. 'But so is injustice. Yes, I am yet to be king, and I do not know what kind of king I will be. But I do have a sense of the kind of Camelot I wish to live in. It would be one where the punishment fits the crime.'

Uther raised an eyebrow defiantly. 'I fear you are right. She has played with fire, and sadly she must die by fire.'

Chapter Ten

Weary and dejected, Merlin opened the door to Gaius' room cautiously and found the physician sitting quietly at one of the tables, as if he'd been waiting for him to return. He looked up as Merlin entered, giving him the briefest of nods, his face saddened and drawn. Then he looked down and sat in silence.

Merlin was surprised. He'd expected to be reprimanded yet again for his folly, but there was none of that this time. Recriminations seemed pointless now; nothing either of them could say would help save Gwen.

Merlin studied Gaius' concerned face, and for the first time in all this, he considered what the old man must be feeling. He'd toiled tirelessly to find a cure, all the while knowing that there were more and more people dying of the disease. And like Merlin, his best efforts had so far come to nothing.

Moving to the window, Merlin looked out over the city. The sky had grown dark, and thick, heavy clouds rolled ominously over Camelot. Moments later they burst open, unleashing torrents of rain on the flimsy dwellings below, as if determined to wash them away.

Merlin couldn't bear the silence any longer. He turned from the window and sat down opposite Gaius. 'I thought I was doing good . . .' he began. 'I thought that curing her father was helping Gwen.' Even as he spoke, the words sounded pitifully inadequate.

Gaius looked up at him. 'I know you acted for the best,' he murmured.

'I thought I was saving a life,' went on Merlin. 'It seemed so simple.'

'An easy solution is like a light in a storm, Merlin,' said Gaius gently. 'Rush for it at your peril, for it may not always lead you to a safe harbour.'

Merlin looked at him. In the half-light, the physician's wrinkled, lined face seemed even more wizened than ever. 'I can see that now,' he nodded.

'How many times have I warned you about the responsibilities of being a warlock?' said Gaius, staring intently into Merlin's eyes. 'Your powers are immense, Merlin, and you must always use them wisely.'

Merlin said nothing, and hung his head. The path ahead of him was more uncertain now than it had ever been. He'd been told countless times what a great destiny awaited him, but right now he doubted if he would ever come to terms with the magical powers he'd been born with. They seemed more of a curse than a gift.

His thoughts turned to Gwen – he could barely comprehend what she must be feeling right now. Then he came to a decision. 'I must see her,' he said, getting up from his chair.

Gaius furrowed his brow in concern. 'I don't think that's going to help either of you, Merlin,' he said. 'There's really nothing you can do for the poor girl now.'

'Maybe there is,' said Merlin determinedly. 'I can't give up. For her sake.'

They were interrupted by a loud knock on the door. The two looked at each other, then Merlin went to open it.

It was Arthur.

Merlin's heart sank, worried he was about to be ordered to run an errand or carry out some menial task. But he couldn't delay. He had to see Gwen.

Luckily it wasn't Merlin that Arthur had come to summon. 'My father is holding an emergency meeting of the privy council,' he said, addressing Gaius. 'He wishes for you to attend immediately.'

'Very well,' said Gaius, rising out of his chair.

Merlin bowed his head to Arthur, muttered an excuse, and sped out of the door before the prince could think of anything else to say.

He quickly made his way to a remote part of the palace he'd visited several times already; a plain, dingy staircase that led down to the palace dungeons deep below the city.

With trepidation, he began to descend, down and down into the gloom, his eyes blinking as they grew accustomed to the darkness. On the way, he suddenly became aware of a slight, hooded figure hurrying up the stairs towards him. He froze, wondering who it could be. The stranger drew nearer and looked up at him sharply in surprise.

It was Morgana, her eyes reddened from her tears.

She barely paused to look at him and hurried straight past, sobbing quietly to herself.

Taking a deep breath, Merlin carried on until eventually he came to the entrance to the dungeon. The guard on duty eyed him suspiciously as he approached, but then looked away, as if considering him no one of any consequence, still less a threat.

Merlin had to stoop a little in order to pass through the doorway, the cold air of the dungeon chilling his bones. There was a rank, musty odour about the place, but there was something much more repellent in the air — it was the ancient smell of fear and hopelessness, of torment and despair. Steeling himself, he looked along the line of cells. Only one, at the far end, was occupied. A dim light came from a feeble, solitary torch.

As he moved cautiously towards the cell, he could just about make out Gwen's form. She was perched awkwardly on a low bench, seemingly oblivious to his presence, her wrists bound in manacles and chains. She seemed broken, lifeless, as she stared in silence at the dank wall of her cell.

Merlin felt another wave of remorse sweep over him and he took a deep breath to try and keep himself together. 'Gwen!' he called softly.

Gwen's head turned towards him, her tears glistening

in the torchlight. At first, there was no flicker of recognition, then her face suddenly lit up and she jumped off the bench towards the cell door. There was a loud chinking sound and Gwen cried out as her chains pulled taut.

'Are you all right?' Merlin gasped, trying to reach out to her through the bars of the cell.

'I'm fine,' said Gwen, nursing her bruised wrists. 'Thank you,' she said, smiling weakly.

'What for?'

'For coming to see me,' she said simply.

Merlin looked down for a moment, finding this impossible. 'I'm sorry ...' he said, looking up at last. 'For everything that's happened to you.'

'It's not your fault,' she said, brushing away his sympathy, tears brimming in her eyes. Merlin couldn't bear it. 'It's all right,' she said. 'Don't worry about me. There's no point in crying about it ...' A startled look passed over her face. 'I mean, I'm not saying you were going to cry about me. Obviously I don't think that ...'

'Oh, Gwen,' murmured Merlin. 'I can't have this happen.'

'Please. One thing ...' said Gwen. 'And you don't have to, but ...' Her voice tailed off, and her brow creased, as if she suddenly thought better of what she'd been about to say.

'What is it?' asked Merlin softly.

She looked up, her wide brown eyes staring at him solemnly. 'Remember me.'

Merlin felt his mouth go dry as he held her gaze. He couldn't take much more. 'You're not going to die,' he said. 'I'm not going to let this happen.'

That was it. Merlin's mind was made up. He turned and bolted out of the dungeon, slipping past the startled guard by the main entrance. He didn't like leaving Gwen like that, but he had to go before she called him back to try and change his mind.

He leaped up the gloomy staircase, taking three full steps at a time, and with his heart pounding in his chest, ran along the palace corridors, not slowing down till he'd reached the council chamber. As usual, two soldiers stood guard outside it and they instinctively crossed their spears in front of him as he came running up to them.

'You can't go in there,' growled one of them. 'The king is not to be disturbed.'

Merlin couldn't believe this. No way was he going to let two stupid guards get in his way now. 'Let me enter!' he insisted, attempting to slip past the makeshift blockade. 'I have an urgent message for King Uther. I mustn't delay.'

'It'll have to wait,' snarled the other guard, grabbing Merlin by the arm and shoving him backwards with ease. 'We have our orders. The king will see no one.'

The guards laughed mockingly at him and Merlin took a step back. He decided to try a different tack. He smiled at them apologetically. 'You're right, I'm sorry, I'll just wait here,' he said meekly. As he stood before the doors he could hear the sound of raised voices coming from inside. He listened hard, trying to make out who was speaking.

'What if burning this witch doesn't stop the poison?' came the sombre tones of the king. 'How do I protect my people?'

'My men have closed down the water pumps,' came another voice, which sounded very much like Arthur's.

'But the emergency supply won't last for much longer,' countered Gaius. 'We have to find a way of cleansing the water of the disease ...'

Merlin couldn't wait any more. He was afraid – so terribly afraid – but there was no choice. He turned his back on the guards so they couldn't see his face, and felt the fire rising inside as he invoked the forces deep within himself. His eyes flared brightly and he spun back round again, hurling himself at the doors with impossible speed. By the time the stunned guards could react, Merlin had already flung open the doors and charged right through.

He was greeted by faces staring at him in complete shock. Not that Merlin cared what people thought any more.

'It was *me*!' he blurted out to the astonished onlookers. 'It was me who used magic to cure Gwen's father. Gwen is not the sorcerer. *I* am!'

Chapter Eleven

For Merlin, it was as if time itself had slowed to a standstill. Gaius, Arthur and the assembled nobles – even the king himself – were gawking at him in disbelief. He was dimly aware of the clatter of armour behind him as the two guards came running in. Uther raised a hand sharply and they held back.

Gaius struck the table with his fist. 'Merlin! Are you *mad*?' he gasped, rising out of his chair.

'I cannot let her die for me,' said Merlin. He looked at Uther, ready to accept his fate. 'I place myself at your mercy, sire.'

Uther stared at Merlin with uncertainty, as if not quite sure what to make of him.

Gaius turned to address him. 'Sire, he doesn't know what he's talking about.'

'I do!' snapped Merlin. No way was he going to allow Gaius to stop him now.

'Then arrest him,' commanded the king, motioning to his guards.

Arthur had been watching the scene playing out in front of him with mounting horror, and as the guards began to manhandle Merlin from the chamber, he finally stirred into life. 'Father, please. This is sheer *madness*!' he scoffed. He strode up to Merlin, waving away the guards. 'There's no way Merlin is a sorcerer.'

'Did you not hear him?' said Uther.

'Well, yes . . .' conceded Arthur.

'He's admitted it.'

'He saved my life, remember?'

Merlin was speechless. It had never occurred to him that his audience wouldn't believe him. But what was even more surprising was how vehemently Arthur was defending him.

'Why should he fabricate such a story?' asked Uther.

'As Gaius said . . .' began Arthur, searching around for the right words. 'He's got a grave *mental* disease . . .'

Merlin gawped at him.

'Really?' said Uther, leaning forward, intrigued at the turn of events.

'Yes,' said Arthur. He gave a short gasp as inspiration struck. 'He's in love . . .'

'What!' said Merlin.

'. . . with Gwen,' finished Arthur.

Uther looked down, trying to suppress a smile.

Merlin was panicking. 'I am not!' he said.

'Yes, you are,' retorted Arthur.

'No way!'

'I saw you yesterday with that flower she'd given you,' Arthur smirked, giving his audience a sly wink.

Merlin cringed, reading the expressions of the people before him. Their horrified looks had now given way to amusement. He'd become their entertainment, a welcome distraction from the horrors of the plague.

'I'm . . . I'm not in love with her . . .' he stammered.

'It's all right, Merlin, you can admit it,' said Arthur with mock pity, and he laid a reassuring arm on his shoulder.

'I don't even think of her like that!' retaliated Merlin, but he knew it was already too late. He could tell from the sniggering faces around him that the image of him as a young, hot-headed romantic was complete in everyone's minds.

Uther leaned forward in his throne, his face unreadable. 'Perhaps she cast a spell on *you*?'

A pause. Merlin didn't know how to take the remark. Then Uther suddenly began to laugh, and the gathered nobles quickly joined in, the whole chamber soon in uproar.

Arthur gave Merlin's head a playful shove. 'Merlin is a wonder,' he said. 'But the wonder is that he's such an *idiot*! There's no way he's a sorcerer.'

With a benign wave of the hand, Uther dismissed Merlin. 'Don't waste my time again,' he said. 'Let him go.'

Merlin looked around, bewildered. He'd failed miserably. Gaius stood up once more and addressed the king. 'If you'll pardon me, sire, my duties are most pressing.'

'Of course, Gaius,' nodded Uther. 'Keep me informed the moment you learn anything.'

The old man bowed graciously, then moved towards the open door, giving Merlin a pointed look to do the same. Merlin duly turned on his heel and left the hall, but as he did so, he felt a hand grab him by the scruff of the neck, propelling him down the corridor. Only when they were back in Gaius' quarters did his mentor let him go.

'I can't believe Arthur had the nerve to call me an idiot in front of all those people,' Merlin muttered, rubbing his sore neck. '*He's* the idiot!'

'No,' said Gaius curtly. 'He was right to do what he did. And you should be thankful he was quick-witted enough to save you from your own stupidity.'

'What else could I do?' asked Merlin desperately. 'It's *my* fault Gwen's going to die.'

'Yes, but you don't prove her innocence by offering to jump into the flames,' snapped Gaius. 'You do it by finding out what's causing the disease. If we can do that, we might yet save her. There's still some hope.'

Merlin was slightly comforted by Gaius' words, but he was still smarting from the dent to his pride. 'Well, whatever it is, one thing's for sure – Arthur's not going to find it. He thinks he's so sharp . . .' Gaius looked at him, waiting for him to finish. '. . . Even when I told him I was a wizard, he still couldn't see it . . .'

Gaius looked him up and down. 'Well, sometimes it's pretty hard to spot.'

'Maybe I should go around wearing a pointy hat,' shrugged Merlin.

'I don't think you'll find one big enough,' shot back

Gaius, allowing himself a rare smile. Merlin was about to reply, but decided to give up.

'Anyway,' continued the old man, 'let's forget all that.' He tossed a large leather bag to Merlin and moved back towards the door.

'Where are we going then?'

'If we're going to save Gwen, we have to find out what it is that's contaminating the water, remember?' said Gaius.

'You think your friend might have found something?' said Merlin.

'Let's hope so,' replied Gaius. 'Come on!'

The two of them hurried off to the Hall of Records, and arrived to find Geoffrey waiting anxiously to see them.

'You're in luck,' said the old man, clutching a grubby scroll tied up with ribbon. 'It took me a long time to find it – I was sure it had been lost!' He rolled out the parchment on his desk.

'So how does this help us?' said Merlin, unable to make head nor tail of the faded lines and symbols on the plans.

'It's quite elementary,' sniffed Geoffrey haughtily, jabbing a finger at a cluster of triangular shapes on the map. 'Water flows down into the valley from these mountains here,' he said. 'The tributaries feed into a large underground stream which courses under Camelot itself, feeding this reservoir here...' His finger traced the line of the underground river and stopped when it reached a large square shape on the map. 'The city hand-pumps draw their supply from this.'

'So where exactly is this reservoir?' frowned Gaius.

'It's in an underground vault outside the city walls,' went on Geoffrey. 'It's accessed via a system of tunnels.' He pointed at the map again. It showed clearly the labyrinthine tunnels leading to the reservoir.

Gaius took the map from his friend, studying it intently. 'So if anyone wanted to poison the water supply, the reservoir is the point they would choose.'

'Well, yes it is, but I really don't see how,' said Geoffrey, scratching his head in puzzlement. 'There is only one door to the vault and I have the key in my safekeeping. No one's been down there...well... for as long as I can remember.'

Gaius rolled up the parchment again. 'Nevertheless, someone's found a way to do it,' he said ominously. 'I think we'd better take a look for ourselves.'

As Gaius collected the key and said goodbye to his friend, Merlin noticed his face was beset with worry. 'What do you think we'll find down there?' asked Merlin.

'I don't know, Merlin,' murmured Gaius, 'but whatever it is, we'd better find it quickly – otherwise it'll be the end of all of us!'

Chapter Twelve

The waters bubbled and rippled, as if something was beginning to stir deep beneath the surface.

Intrigued, the woman peered into the pool, wondering what vision it would offer up next. Through the restless, churning waters, the image was cloudy, indistinct, and all she could make out was a brilliant white light and the shimmering silhouettes of two figures. She closed her eyes and concentrated, her pale hand sweeping over the waters' surface.

'*Show me . . .*' she whispered.

The waters frothed and effervesced in obedience, and the woman looked into them again. One of the figures had sharpened into focus and she recognized the likeness immediately; a stooped old man, with long, matted grey hair, dressed in voluminous orange robes. The woman gave a snort of derision.

She had no time for that senile old fool, Gaius. A man who claimed to know so much, yet in reality knew nothing.

But what of the other figure?

Her eyes looked at it expectantly, but the silhouette remained darkened and blurred, as if unwilling to reveal its identity. The woman glared at the pool. '*I said show me!*' she hissed.

The waters bubbled and swirled ever more violently, and as they subsided the second figure swam into focus at last. The woman was less than impressed. It was just the face of a boy with wide-set eyes and a mop of black hair. He was standing at the top of a flight of stone steps, staring into the darkness like some startled animal. How endearingly pathetic.

But wait . . .

There was something about him, she could feel it. She held out her hand and caressed the surface of the water. The image of the boy broke up into myriad shimmering fragments.

The woman gave a startled gasp and snatched her hand away. Her eyes narrowed as the waters became still once more, the image reassembling itself on the surface. She studied the figure more intently. There was certainly more to this guileless youth than met the eye – the waters had indicated as much.

She stared at him, sensing a churning inner turmoil, his feeble young mind confused by a thousand thoughts and conflicting emotions, all of which made him difficult to read.

But through all of this, two things became clear; the unmistakable sense of a dark truth kept hidden and the promise of greatness yet to come.

The woman smiled. The boy was an enigma, one she was determined to learn more about. But her mind shifted to more pressing matters. The waters had shown Gaius and the boy entering the underground vault, and it was obvious what their intentions were. Closing her eyes once more, she reached out with her mind and linked it with that of the creature, making it aware of the threat posed by the intruders. They had to be stopped, or her great plan would be in jeopardy. The creature let out a long, guttural growl and the woman was satisfied her commands had been understood.

Her fingers stroked the waters' surface once more and the image of Gaius and the boy faded away.

As Merlin descended the steps into the vault, the blackness seemed to swallow up the light from their only torch and the atmosphere felt icy cold. He couldn't help but wonder what they were going to find in the reservoir.

Then he remembered Gwen, thought of her loneliness and despair, how little time she had left, and he willed himself to concentrate on the task in hand. For now at least, he had to be strong and help Gaius any way he could.

'Which way?' he asked, peering into the gloom.

Gaius squinted. 'Forward, I think.'

They moved off, and Merlin imagined they'd reach the underground reservoir in no time. But as they pressed deeper and deeper into the vault, their progress became ever slower. The roof of the tunnel was low in places, forcing them to stoop over as they moved along. Not only that, the rocky floor was often slippery and uneven.

Mercifully, at various points the tunnels would widen out into high chambers, with several other tunnels leading off them. At every such junction point, Merlin noticed an unused torch hanging from the rock wall, and he dutifully lit each one as he came to it. As far as he was concerned, the more light he could bring to this hellhole, the better.

Making their way in silence, they eventually found

themselves in a narrow passageway, so tight for space they had no choice but to walk in single file, Merlin lighting the way with his torch. He felt a growing sense of unease as he walked through the cramped tunnel, compounded by the sensation of claustrophobia.

'Have we got far to go now?' he queried breathlessly.

'I think we're almost there,' came the reply.

To Merlin's relief, the passageway opened out into another chamber. Gaius sat down on a convenient boulder, grateful for a few minutes' rest.

'Are you all right?' Merlin asked at last.

'Yes, I'm fine,' nodded Gaius. 'Just needed to get my breath back, that's all.'

The old man held out his arm and Merlin helped him to his feet. He was beginning to wonder how wise it had been to enter the tunnel system alone. At least with Arthur by their side, they'd have stood a better chance of fending off a possible attack.

'Right, come along, we can't go back now,' said the physician determinedly. He set off down one of the tunnels and Merlin followed close behind him. Thankfully, the passageways were much easier to move through from this point on, and not long afterwards, they found themselves in an enormous cavern seemingly carved out of solid rock, a darkened alcove at the far end.

'This is the place,' said Gaius, his voice echoing in the chamber.

'I can't see the reservoir,' said Merlin, peering into the darkness. 'Actually I can't really see *anything.*'

'Try lighting the torches,' suggested Gaius.

Merlin didn't want to contemplate the possibility that they were lost and he moved round the edge of the chamber, lighting each torch in turn. As the cave became dimly illuminated, he found he could now see into the alcove. It housed a pool of water, in front of which was a low, man-made wall about three feet high, with some stone steps leading up to the edge.

'The water from here supplies the whole town,' said the old man. 'Take a sample – there's a phial in the bag. I'll hold the torch.'

Merlin peered all around, wondering if the sorcerer was watching them at that very moment, about to cast some unspeakable spell on them both. Then he took the phial out of the bag and leaned over the side of the pool, gasping as he put his hand in the water. He hadn't expected it to be so cold. As he filled up the receptacle, he could have sworn he felt a strange swirling movement against his skin. He pulled his hand away and stood back, staring expectantly into the murky depths. There was nothing. He took one last look at the pool, then set off after Gaius.

Suddenly there was an almighty roar behind him.

He spun round.

Some vast shape had burst through the surface of the pool, sending gallons of water cascading over the sides of the wall, almost knocking Merlin and Gaius off their feet.

Merlin stared at it in horror.

It was a hideous sinewy creature some ten feet tall with a large head and lethal claws. It opened its mouth wide and let out a hellish, bloodcurdling scream, revealing a set of terrifying razor-sharp teeth.

Mesmerized by the monstrous sight, Merlin tried desperately to think of a spell to protect them both as the creature reared high above them, screeching and bellowing with rage.

Chapter Thirteen

Another wave of water surged over Merlin and the screeching suddenly stopped.

The creature had vanished.

'What the hell was *that*?' gasped Merlin.

'I don't know, but I have some nasty suspicions,' murmured Gaius, eyeing the pool uncertainly. 'Come on, let's get out of here before it comes back.'

They left the cavern and set off through the labyrinth. 'I don't understand,' Merlin said as they stumbled along in the darkness. 'Why did it rear up at us like that, then just disappear again?'

'Perhaps when you disturbed the water its instinct was simply to scare us off, defend its territory,' replied Gaius breathlessly.

'But it could have torn us to bits!'

'I know . . .' said Gaius. 'Fortunately for us, it doesn't

appear to be the most intelligent of creatures. On this occasion it was simply sizing us up. Next time round, it may not be quite so benign.'

'Next time?' repeated Merlin.

Gaius stopped and turned to face him. 'Well, if we manage to kill the beast, we'll surely end the contamination. It sounds simple, but I only wish we knew how to do it . . .'

Without another word, the two hurried back through the tunnels, and when they finally reached the entrance to the vault, Merlin gave a sigh of relief, glad to be back in the open air at last.

But there was no time to rest.

Minutes later, they were back in Gaius' chambers, and the physician immediately began to climb the rickety staircase that led to a shelf at the very top of the room.

'Which book are you looking for?' called Merlin.

'It's got to be here somewhere,' grunted Gaius, 'but I can't remember where I put it. I don't think I've looked at it for about twenty years.'

He started rummaging around the sagging shelves, breaking into occasional coughing fits as clouds of centuries-old dust enveloped him. Merlin wanted to help, but his mentor's erratic filing system only confused him. Better to let him get on with it.

'Ah-ha!' exclaimed Gaius at last, and he pulled a large tome from the topmost shelf. 'I knew I still had it!' He came hobbling down the stairs, flicking through the crinkled, yellowing leaves till he found what he was looking for. He set the book down on the table. 'There!' he said, with a triumphant jab of his finger. 'It was an *Afanc*!'

'An Af . . . *what*?' Merlin squinted at the page, and his eye was quickly drawn to the crude image of a hunchbacked creature standing on all fours. There was no suggestion of any eyes as such, only a large gash for a mouth – a mouth which was lined with vicious, serrated teeth. It was very similar to the beast they'd seen in the vault. 'So what does it say?' he frowned, wishing he could read the copperplate handwriting, which unfortunately was all in Latin.

'It's a beast born of clay,' translated Gaius, 'which can only be conjured up by the most powerful sorcerer.' He paused, agitatedly sucking the air through his teeth. 'Now we have to find a way to defeat it.'

'Well, doesn't it tell you in there?'

'No, no mention at all,' said Gaius, reading quickly to the end of the page. He snapped the book shut and looked up at the dozens of creaking shelves which lined the room. 'I'm sure we'll find the answer somewhere,' he said. 'But I confess I've really no idea where to start. We'll have to do some research.'

Merlin stared at him. 'That could take us days,' he said. 'Gwen will be dead by then!'

'Have you got a better idea?'

Merlin didn't reply. He'd thought of something – a faint hope of finding the answer – but there was no way he felt able to share his thoughts. He'd have to see this one through on his own.

Muttering some half-hearted excuse under his breath, he left the room and sped out of the palace, making straight for the great square.

The sight that greeted him made his heart stop.

There was a huge pile of wood in the middle of the courtyard; a group of workmen were diligently stacking more sticks and branches on top of it. There was only one purpose it could possibly serve.

It was a pyre for burning witches.

Merlin stared in silent fury as they worked, his hands clenched tightly. He wanted to scream at them to stop, to smash down the pyre, but he willed himself to run past it, heading to the far side of the square. Back inside again, he soon found himself descending the steps that led to the dungeon, trying all the while to put the image of the pyre out of his mind.

The guard on duty barely registered his presence as he made his way to the cells. In the guttering torchlight he could barely see anything at all, and for a moment was worried that Gwen had been taken somewhere else. As his eyes quickly adjusted though, he could just about make out the back of her huddled form on the cold floor, cushioned only by a scattering of filthy straw.

'Gwen?' he called softly.

He paused, waiting for a response. No sign of any movement.

Merlin thought she might be asleep and considered waking her, but he decided it was probably kinder not to.

He was about go when he noticed her body quivering slightly, and heard the faintest of sobs. Wishing desperately for a way to comfort her, he grasped the bars of the cell, pressing his face right up to them. 'Gwen, I'm going to get you out,' he called, as loudly as he dared. 'I *will . . .*'

Again there was no reply, and Merlin wondered whether he should have said anything at all. What if he didn't manage to save her? What right did he have to raise her hopes like that? He gazed down at Gwen's trembling figure and imagined what must be going through her mind. She'd been branded a sorceress, had drawn the unmitigated scorn of nobles and townspeople alike, and now she was facing certain death. It was clear she'd lost all hope.

Merlin turned away. There was only one chance left for him now. He had to concentrate on that.

He crept silently back to the entrance, spying a solitary guard. His back was to him. Merlin cursed under his breath. He needed to get to a door on the other side of the antechamber, but there was no way he could do so without being seen. He looked around for a distraction, and his eyes settled on a torch burning brightly on the wall next to the soldier. Merlin stared at it keenly and felt the energy stirring within him. His eyes flashed immediately and the torch lifted itself out of its holder and clattered onto the hard floor.

Startled, the guard leaped to one side, letting out a cry. He gazed uncertainly at the fallen torch for a moment or two, then gingerly bent down to pick it up. He turned to replace it in its mount and Merlin seized his chance, slipping straight past him. There was another torch on the far wall, and Merlin casually grabbed it before darting through the door.

So far, so good. But that had been the easy bit.

Tentatively he started down a long flight of steps that

seemed to lead into a black nothingness. He'd made this journey several times before, but he was still glad of the reassuring glow from his torch.

He came to the bottom of the steps and found himself in a cramped passageway, the glow of a pale bluish light just visible at the end of it. Merlin headed towards it. As he finally passed through the mouth of the tunnel, he came to a standstill, gawking in wonder at his surroundings.

He was in an underground cavern, so indescribably immense he felt overawed and utterly lost within it. Above him, massive shards of rock hung down like ancient spears, while tall, craggy pillars soared upwards as if to support the vast arched roof. The cavern was suffused with a hazy blue glow, but there was no evidence of any light source, a mystery that only added to the overwhelming sense of strangeness and wonder.

But right now, Merlin had more important things on his mind.

He was standing on a ledge of rock which jutted out over the yawning chasm, and he slowly inched forward, peering over the edge into the blackness.

There was nothing there.

'Hello?' he called, trying his best to keep calm.

Suddenly a shadow caught his eye high above him, and he could hear the sound of flapping wings as a shape came swooping down towards him.

'Hello!' boomed back a mighty voice, resonating all around the cavern.

Instinctively Merlin took a few paces back as a huge creature settled on the ridge of rocks some distance in front of him. Many times the size of a man, it had expansive leathery wings and a lithe, sinewy body covered in shiny golden scales.

This was the Great Dragon, the very last of its kind.

It fixed its large, beady eyes on Merlin as it folded its wings against its body. 'Well, the great warlock returns, as I knew he would,' it rasped.

Merlin rubbed the side of his skull. When the Dragon spoke, its booming voice somehow sounded like it was coming from all around him – even inside his head. It was a very strange feeling.

'I need to know how to defeat an Afanc,' he stammered, deciding to come straight to the point.

'Yes, I suppose you do,' said the creature airily, its great mouth parted in a half-smile.

Merlin stared at it, unsure what to make of the remark. Since he'd arrived in Camelot, the Dragon had told him much about the future, about the purpose of his magical powers, and of his great destiny as Arthur's protector. He'd learned that the creature had long ago been imprisoned by Uther in his quest to purge the kingdom of all magic, and Merlin had no doubt the beast possessed wisdom way beyond the experience of mere mortals.

But despite all that, it had the irksome habit of talking in riddles, and Merlin wasn't entirely convinced he could trust it.

'Will you help me?' he said at last.

The Dragon's golden eyes narrowed as it considered his question. 'Trust the elements that are at your command,' it boomed.

'Elements?' repeated Merlin. 'But what is it I have to do?'

The dragon leaned closer. 'You cannot do this alone,' it said. 'You are but one side of a coin. Arthur is the other.'

Merlin shook his head. 'I don't understand. Just tell me! What is it I have to do?' he said desperately, but the Dragon had already unfurled its great wings, preparing to launch itself into the air once more. 'No!' yelled Merlin. 'Please, help me!'

'I have . . .' the beast remarked playfully as it leaped

from the ridge, flapping its wings in earnest. Merlin could only stand and watch it rise steadily upwards, a lasting chuckle echoing about the rocky walls as it lost itself in the vastness of the cavern.

Crushed, Merlin closed his eyes tightly. 'Yeah, right. Thanks,' he whispered to himself. Gwen's face flashed into his mind, and all he could think about was the hollow promise he'd made. He'd come to the Dragon for answers, but as ever all he was left with was a puzzle.

And he hadn't the faintest idea how to solve it.

Chapter Fourteen

Uther was lost in thought as he stood alone in the council chamber, staring vacantly at the dancing flame of a solitary candle. There were marks etched into the stem at regular intervals, which seemed to be counting down the hours till Gwen's death. By tomorrow night the witch would be dead, and Camelot would be released from her accursed plague. Or so Uther hoped.

Suddenly the doors to the chamber swung open, and the delicate flame guttered for a moment, almost extinguished in the sudden draught.

'Father?' Arthur's voice was soft, respectful.

Uther barely noted his presence. He was still contemplating the candle, the flame having recovered, burning as brightly as ever. 'Have you found anything more?' he murmured.

'I've tried,' began Arthur. 'I can keep looking . . .' He broke off as Uther turned to face him. He was struck by his father's weariness, the sallowness of his skin.

'People are still dying,' said Uther, shaking his head. 'We can't delay any longer.' He leaned over the candle and blew it out, watching as a thin plume of smoke rose up into the air.

Arthur frowned. 'What do you want me to do, Father?'

'We must kill the witch. Bring her execution forward to tonight.'

Arthur was about to object, but he changed his mind. After all, there was nothing more he could do. With a gracious bow, he left his father, the great doors clanging shut behind him. Grim-faced, he marched off down the passageway.

Without warning, a figure sprung out of the shadows to block his path.

It was Morgana.

Arthur avoided her gaze. The last thing he was in the mood for was a confrontation.

'Any news?' asked Morgana, searching Arthur's face intently.

The prince shook his head. 'There's no point

looking any more, Morgana. We've done all we can.'

Her eyes flashed. 'So you think Gwen's the sorceress after all?'

'I didn't say that . . .'

'Then what do you mean?' snapped Morgana. 'Why've you given up the search?'

Arthur rolled his eyes, bowing to the inevitable. The truth would be out soon anyway. 'My father wants her executed tonight.'

Morgana's face twisted in contempt and she pushed past him, heading for the council chamber. Arthur caught her arm just in time.

'It's no good,' he warned. 'Really. My father's made up his mind, and with the state he's in, I really wouldn't go antagonizing him. It isn't worth it.'

Morgana shook Arthur's hand away angrily, and her eyes misted over. 'So that's it then?' she said bitterly. 'I'm supposed to stand by and watch while Gwen is burned alive?'

'Morgana, please . . .'

Stifling a sob, Morgana ran off down the darkened passageway. Arthur thought about going after her, but then remembered himself. He had his duty to carry out.

★

Meanwhile, Merlin had returned to Gaius' chambers, but instead of finding the old man hard at work, he'd discovered he was nowhere to be seen.

Quickly he set about hefting Gaius' books from the buckling shelves, and began skimming through one grubby tome after another. He became utterly absorbed in his task, and when Gaius eventually returned, he hardly even looked up.

'Merlin, what are you doing?' asked the physician.

'Looking for a book . . .' said Merlin absently.

'Are you going to tell me which one?' Gaius set his bag down.

'I need a book on the elements . . .'

'The elements?'

'Yes. Which one would I find them in?'

'Well, most of them,' said Gaius. 'The study of base elements is at the very heart of the scientific process.'

'Base elements?' echoed Merlin blankly.

'Yes – earth, fire, wind and water.'

'Oh.' Merlin's face fell.

'What exactly do you want to know about them?' asked Gaius, his curiosity roused.

'I was just wondering how they might help me defeat the Afanc,' said Merlin, suddenly noticing a pile of books about to topple over and rushing to steady them.

Gaius concentrated. 'Well, the Afanc is a creature made from earth and water, that's two of the four base elements . . .'

'So what about the other two?'

'Well, perhaps they might destroy it . . .' mused Gaius. Suddenly a look of realization flashed across his face. 'Yes, that's it, Merlin. You want fire. Wind and fire!'

Merlin felt a glimmer of hope. Unbelievably he'd managed to make sense of the Dragon's cryptic words and discover how to destroy the creature. Now all he had to do was find the thing again and kill it. Simple.

'Erm, how did you find all this out, by the way?' Gaius was looking at him, a trace of suspicion in his voice.

Merlin's mind raced. 'Erm, I just knew, you know? Part of my powers.'

'Oh. What else do your powers tell you?'

Merlin stared into the middle distance as if delving into the fathomless depths of his subconscious. 'They tell me that I'm only one side of a coin,' he said mysteriously. 'The brighter side, obviously.'

'And who's the other side?'

'I think that might be Arthur,' replied Merlin, momentarily amused by his mentor's astonished reaction.

Just then, the chamber door burst open and Morgana came rushing in, desperation on her face. 'They're bringing forward the execution,' she said. 'We have to prove Gwen's innocence or she'll die tonight.'

'We're trying,' said Gaius. 'Merlin thinks he knows . . .' His voice tailed off suddenly, as if worried about giving too much away to someone so close to the king.

'Please,' she said, giving both of them a beseeching look. 'Just tell me what I can do to help.'

'We need Arthur,' said Merlin simply.

'*Arthur?*' Morgana did little to disguise her surprise.

'There's a monster — an Afanc — in the water supply,' explained Merlin. 'That's what's causing the plague.'

Morgana was appalled. 'Well, we must tell Uther!'

Gaius shook his head. 'An Afanc is a creature forged by magic. Telling Uther wouldn't save Gwen, he'd just blame her for conjuring it.'

Morgana's face clouded in despair. 'So what are we to do?'

'We need to destroy it, then the plague will stop,' said Merlin eagerly. 'And Uther *may* see sense.'

Morgana curled her lip. 'Well, we can hope. And you need Arthur to help kill the creature?'

'He's our best chance,' said Merlin. 'But he won't want to disobey the king.'

Morgana pondered this for a moment, then fixed Merlin with a determined look. 'Leave that to me.' She turned on her heel and hurried out of the door.

Gaius handed Merlin the keys to the underground vault, then Merlin bounded up the steps to his room. He took the book of magic from its hiding place, set it on his bed and began to look through it for the right spell.

'Wind and fire, wind and fire . . .' he muttered under his breath as he searched frantically through the pages. He thought carefully about how he'd need to master both elements in order to destroy the creature. They would need a torch anyway to see in the vault, so the fire part was easy. But to gain control of the air itself, to summon a great wind in the confines of the caves . . . he'd need a very powerful spell to do that.

He thought back to the last time he'd used magic to save Arthur's life, how he'd sat up all night trying desperately to get a difficult spell to work. He remembered repeating the incantation over and over a thousand times until eventually – and it had to be said, accidentally – he'd discovered the exact inflections that had unlocked the power of the magic words.

But this time he had no such luxury. He had just a few minutes to learn the spell, and that was it. No time to practise, and no room for mistakes. If they faced the Afanc and his magic failed, they'd all be dead for certain.

In another part of the palace, Morgana had already found Arthur alone in his chambers. He'd been trying to take a few minutes' rest after issuing the guards with their orders.

'Are you all right?' he frowned, suddenly noticing a downcast-looking Morgana standing in his room.

Morgana didn't reply and simply stared at the floor in silence. Arthur cleared his throat and looked around for a distraction. The large table in the centre of the room caught his attention. Its surface was littered with the leftovers of several meals – stale crusts of bread, gnawed bones, browning apple cores – not to mention food that had already rotted away to the point where it could no longer be identified. 'Sorry about all this,' he coughed again. 'Merlin's not been in.'

'Poor Merlin,' murmured Morgana.

'Yeah,' said Arthur, half-heartedly beginning to clear up.

'He offered to give up his life for Gwen's...' Morgana went on with a melancholic air. 'I certainly can't imagine any man loving me so much.'

Arthur stopped what he was doing and turned to her. It wasn't like Morgana to pour out her heart to him. 'No, I certainly can't imagine that either,' he said.

'That's because you're not like Merlin,' said Morgana, a sly smile playing across her lips. 'He's a lover.'

'Well, maybe that's because I haven't found the right person to love,' said Arthur, not at all sure where this was heading. Morgana's despairing words were curiously at odds with the cunning glint in her eye. He knew she was up to something, but somehow he felt compelled to play along with her.

'Sadly the age of gallantry seems to be dead,' Morgana continued. 'You look around and all you see are small men not big enough to fill their armour. There's not one of them who's able to stand up for what is right...'

Arthur smiled and held up his hand in defeat, impressed by how expertly manipulated he'd been. 'All right, what do you want me to do?'

Morgana's expression changed suddenly and she became deadly serious. 'Gaius and Merlin say there's some creature beneath the city causing the disease,' she said. 'We need to find it and kill it—'

'Hang on,' cut in Arthur, staring at her in disbelief. 'What *are* you talking about?'

'Please . . .' she said. 'You have to help us. It's Gwen's last chance.'

Arthur looked into her wide eyes with uncertainty. He had no idea whether to believe her or not.

Chapter Fifteen

'*Where have they got to?*' Merlin muttered under his breath as he waited impatiently in the palace square for Morgana and Arthur to appear. What if Morgana failed to persuade him to help? A shiver ran through his body and he pulled his coat tighter about him. He tried not to think about facing the terrifying beast alone, his only protection a spell he'd never even tried. He glanced around the square for something to take his mind off things.

It offered precious little comfort.

Right in the middle of the courtyard stood the finished pyre, two stony-faced soldiers standing guard by it. In just a matter of hours it would be set ablaze. Merlin closed his eyes tightly, determined to blot them out, but a blur of terrifying images was already flashing in front of him – Gwen dragged in chains before the baying crowd, the king's cold, hateful face as he pronounced judgement; Gwen's screams as she—

'What are you doing?'

His eyes snapped open. Arthur was striding towards him, Morgana a few paces behind. Merlin grinned at them in relief, scarcely believing that Morgana had actually done it.

'So what's this monster like?' asked Arthur as he drew nearer.

'It's, um, huge . . .' began Merlin, thinking back to his encounter in the cavern. 'With big teeth and claws.'

Arthur looked unconvinced, but said nothing more.

The three of them left the city, Arthur and Morgana following as Merlin went directly to the door that led down to the tunnels. Merlin unlocked it and felt an icy draught on his face as it creaked open. He recoiled instinctively, then noticed Arthur and Morgana looking at him.

'Are you up to this?' asked Arthur dubiously.

'I'm fine,' Merlin replied. 'Just a bit chilly, that's all.'

He went to step through the doorway, but Arthur held up his arm and entered first. There was a blazing torch just inside it, and the prince lit one for himself and one for Morgana.

'Ready?' Arthur said.

'Yes,' Merlin nodded, and they carefully began to make their way down the steps into the tunnels beyond. For a while they made good progress – until they came to a junction point and an unexpected fork in the passageway.

'Hold on a moment . . .' Merlin stopped dead and looked around them.

'What is it?' said Arthur. 'Are we lost?'

Merlin shook his head. 'I don't understand. I remember the tunnel branching off in three directions at this point. I was expecting to bear right.'

'So we *are* lost,' muttered Arthur.

'Well, no . . . I don't know . . .' stammered Merlin, wondering how they could have gone wrong.

'I thought you said you'd been down here before?'

Morgana stepped between them and shot Arthur a warning look. 'Just leave him for a moment,' she said. 'I'm sure he'll pick up the trail again.'

Merlin racked his brains and realized he must have just mis-remembered the route. 'I think we take the left fork here,' he said at last.

'Are you sure?' said Arthur.

'Yes,' Merlin nodded, not sure at all.

'You'd better be right about this, Merlin,' said the prince, and the three of them moved off once more. They'd barely gone any distance at all when a low, guttural roar made them all freeze in their tracks. Arthur drew his sword. 'That came from up ahead somewhere,' he breathed, peering into the darkness. Grim-faced, he turned to Morgana. 'You should stay here,' he ordered.

'I'm coming with you.' Morgana fixed him with a determined stare.

'No!'

'Scared I'll show you up?'

'Father would slam us both in chains if he knew I'd endangered you!' Arthur insisted.

'Good thing he doesn't know about it then,' said Morgana.

Merlin glanced at his master. He could see he was trying his best to keep calm, but Morgana had an expert way of needling him.

'I'm telling you, Morgana, turn back,' Arthur said. 'You could get hurt!'

'So could you' – she smiled sweetly – 'if you don't get out of my way.'

She pushed past Arthur. Merlin gave him a consolatory smile, and they hurried after her, the three of them pressing deeper and deeper into the labyrinth.

'How are we going to find it?' whispered Morgana.

'Just hope we do before it finds us,' said Merlin matter-of-factly.

Suddenly they heard another primal roar echoing in the darkness. Alarmed, Arthur looked behind him for some sign of the creature.

'Where's it coming from?' whispered Merlin. 'I can't tell . . .'

He looked back down the passage they'd just walked along, straining his eyes. He was sure he could see a small movement in the distance, but in the dimness of the flickering torchlight, it was difficult to be sure.

'It's all right,' said Arthur, reading his expression. 'It's just a shadow.'

They set off again and Merlin recognized the part of the tunnel they were in – not too much further to go now. But as they walked along, he sensed the tunnels were becoming warmer – and ever more airless – with every step. He loosened his scarf a little and a nasty thought struck him – what if there was more than one

Afanc? Surely if the sorcerer could summon one such creature, he could conjure up others just as easily? Merlin mulled over this chilling possibility in his mind as they walked past a tunnel opening to their right. Without warning, there was yet another terrifying roar.

The creature was right on top of them.

Arthur spun round, brandishing his sword, preparing for the beast to pounce. Merlin's heart thumped in his chest and he grabbed Morgana's arm, twisting her backwards out of the way.

But nothing happened.

'Bring the other torch here, Merlin,' snapped Arthur. Merlin obeyed and moved to his side, the two flickering flames lighting the opening to the tunnel. 'There must have been something there,' said Arthur angrily.

'It's just playing with us,' said Morgana, 'trying to scare us so we start making mistakes.'

Arthur glared madly at the darkness. 'All I want is an honest fight!' he yelled. 'So why don't you show yourself?'

Merlin patted his arm. 'Come on,' he said. 'There's nothing there now, and the cavern's just round the next bend.'

Arthur waited just a moment longer, as if expecting

the creature to suddenly appear, then he gave up and turned to join the others.

Moments later, the three of them finally entered the huge chamber and Merlin gave a gasp of relief, glad to be out of the stifling tunnels. He looked up at the cavern walls and realized that the torches he'd lit earlier had all gone out. He stared at them in disbelief. Could it be the creature wasn't quite as stupid as Gaius had thought?

Arthur crossed over to the reservoir on the far side of the cavern and peered warily into the darkened pool. 'This is where you saw it?' he said.

'Yes,' said Merlin, moving to join him. 'I wouldn't get too close if I were you.'

As he spoke, something caught his eye at the edge of the pool – a jagged white shape floating on the water's surface. He bent down to pick it up.

'What's that?' asked Morgana.

'I don't know . . .' Merlin handed her the torch and picked up the object. He turned it over in his hands, examining it. 'It looks like a piece of eggshell,' he said. He stuffed it into his bag without a further thought.

'Never mind that,' said Arthur. 'Tell me what you saw again.'

Merlin frowned. 'It just came up at us, then disappeared back under the water. Gaius thought it might be protecting its territory.'

'Did he?' Arthur bit his lip. 'Well, that might be just what we need . . .'

He bent down and picked up a big boulder from the cave floor, hefting the weight of it in his hands. Without warning, he whirled round and hurled the rock into the reservoir with all his strength. It made a deafening splash which echoed all around the cavern.

'What are you doing?' gasped Merlin.

'Simple – I'm invading its territory,' said Arthur. 'If it's heard the noise, it should come running. Then we can kill it!'

As the echo subsided, he turned to Morgana and Merlin. 'Right, you two, spread out, see what else we can find.'

The others obeyed and began searching the farthest corners of the cavern. As Merlin edged his way round the perimeter he noticed a dim recess in the wall – yet another tunnel leading off the chamber. He looked around to see where Morgana had got to, but he couldn't make out the light from her torch. She must have found another tunnel too.

Suddenly he heard a startled cry behind him, followed

by a terrifying, ear-splitting screech. He spun round and saw Arthur in the distance by the edge of the pool, the Afanc bearing down on him. As the prince swung his sword wildly to defend himself, the creature's mighty claws came slicing down, knocking the torch from his hand, extinguishing the flame.

The whole cavern was plunged into darkness.

Chapter Sixteen

Without thinking, Merlin darted towards Arthur. He could only guess where he was going and he suddenly slammed into a heavy shape in the darkness. There was a strangled yell and something punched him in the stomach, knocking him backwards with terrifying force. He stumbled and fell, winded and dazed.

There came the sound of running footsteps and Morgana appeared, carrying her torch. 'What is it? Are you all right?' she cried, seeing Merlin and Arthur sprawled on the cave floor, rubbing their aching limbs.

'Merlin, what were you doing?' yelled Arthur, getting to his feet. 'I could have cut your head off!'

Merlin looked around for the creature. 'Where did it go?' he said, hauling himself up.

'It's quick,' said Arthur, catching his breath and using

Morgana's torch to relight his own. 'From now on, we'd better stick together.'

And so they stood and waited in silence, looking around expectantly, wondering when the next strike would come. Merlin's eyes darted about the cavern, his senses alert to the slightest sound, the tiniest movement, that would give warning of another attack.

Despite the danger, his thoughts began to wander. With the creature able to move so fast, he wondered how he'd get close enough to make the spell work. And what if Arthur or Morgana saw him using his magic? Could he really trust them not to tell the king?

Suddenly a piercing scream shattered the silence. He whirled round to see the hulking form of the Afanc bearing down on Morgana, its savage jaws snapping at her as she tried to duck out of the way. She thrust her torch into the creature's face and it let out a hellish screech as it recoiled, tearing wildly at the flames.

'Get out of the way, Morgana!' shouted Arthur, bringing his sword down hard on the creature's skull. But instead of wounding it, the blade simply rebounded off the beast's skin, like it was made of solid stone. Horrified, Arthur drew back as the furious creature lashed out at him with its claws. He swung his sword at it again, but the Afanc had already disappeared in a blur of movement, back to the cover of the shadows.

'Where is it?' Arthur's eyes darted around the cavern.

Merlin heard a low, rumbling growl somewhere in the tunnel behind him and turned round to look. 'I think it's gone this way!' he called, and the three of them hurried across to the opening, the snarling noise becoming louder with every step.

As Merlin edged into the passageway, he could see a dim shadow some thirty feet ahead of them. He couldn't make out the Afanc's features, but he had a nasty feeling it was watching them, studying their every move, waiting for another chance to strike. It seemed more confident now, like it no longer felt the need to attack by stealth.

Merlin moved as close to it as he dared. He could smell the Afanc's rank breath in the passageway, like the stench of rotting meat. He watched as Arthur inched nearer to the creature. With every step, Merlin realized time was running out. The creature would obey its instinct and kill every one of them.

If he was going to use his magic at all, then this would be his only chance.

By now, Arthur was so close Merlin could see the

outline of the Afanc and the fiery glow of the prince's torch reflected in its glistening skin. The creature growled at the prince furiously like a rabid animal, shifting its weight restlessly from one paw to another as it skulked in the shadows.

'What are you waiting for?' breathed Morgana. 'Just kill it!'

The tension was unbearable, but Merlin could see what Arthur was doing. He was getting as close to it as possible, to give himself the best chance of making the perfect strike.

Merlin's eyes never left the creature. It fell silent, and moved back onto its haunches ready to spring forward. Anticipating its movement, the prince brought his sword down heavily on the beast, catching it a glancing blow on the side of its head. The Afanc hissed in anger and reared up, lashing out at him. Arthur dodged nimbly to one side, then began swiping and slashing at the creature's body, determined to find a weak spot in its toughened skin.

The beast parried his blows savagely and slowly began to force the prince backwards. Arthur tried desperately to regain the advantage, but the Afanc was immensely powerful, fending off every sword blow with ease, howling at him in anger.

As Merlin watched, he could see Arthur's stamina was starting to wane, while the creature's fearsome strength showed no sign of abating. With his back almost against the tunnel wall, Arthur made a last wild attempt to stab the Afanc in the chest. The creature let out a shriek of pain and lashed out at the sword, wrenching it from Arthur's grasp. It fell to the ground with a clatter, skittering out of reach.

'Arthur!' yelled Merlin. 'Use the torch!'

Instinctively Arthur thrust the flaming torch in the Afanc's misshapen face. It reared up on its back legs and let out a deafening, bloodcurdling screech, holding up its sinewy arms to protect itself from the heat. Morgana's face contorted in horror at the hideous sight before her.

With all eyes on the creature, Merlin knew this was his chance.

It was now or never.

He held up his hand and murmured the incantation under his breath. '*Lyfte ic pe in balwen ac forhienan se wideor!*' He reached deep inside, summoning all his power, feeling it coursing through his veins.

His eyes flashed intensely and a great rushing sound filled the tunnels, followed by a mighty wind which blew fiercely all around them. Morgana and Arthur were almost knocked off their feet, but Merlin barely noticed it. It was like he was standing in the eye of a storm.

He concentrated hard. Suddenly the tip of Arthur's torch seemed to explode and the flames fanned outwards, a great fireball arcing towards the creature. Arthur turned his head away as the Afanc became engulfed in flames, screaming and twisting in torment, the blistering heat already melting away its flesh.

'Everyone back!' yelled Arthur, and he ran towards Morgana and Merlin, pushing them into the safety of the cavern. Merlin watched the creature's last moments, holding up his arm to shield himself from the inferno. With a last pitiful, dying roar, the Afanc slumped to the ground, its body blackened and shrunken. The fire raged fiercely and the creature became still at last.

'What was *that*?' cried Arthur, gasping for breath and turning to Merlin.

'Dunno . . .' Merlin tried his best to look innocent. 'Must be freak air currents in the tunnels or something. I'll have to ask Gaius about it . . .' He held his breath, waiting for a reply. He knew his explanation didn't sound remotely plausible. He just hoped Arthur wouldn't press him any further.

But Arthur just shook his head dismissively and looked back into the tunnel. 'Who cares?' he murmured.

'The thing's dead. That's all that matters.'

Merlin breathed easily again, watching the creature burn with a mixture of revulsion and relief. The magic had worked and the plague was surely at an end. But as he stared at the charred remains of the Afanc, it seemed a hollow victory somehow. The beast had been nothing more than a victim itself, the mindless slave of some evil sorcerer. A sorcerer who was still alive.

'It's all over,' said Arthur, sheathing his sword.

'Not quite,' said Morgana, already hurrying out of the cavern. 'You're forgetting Gwen. We've still got to stop the execution!'

Chapter Seventeen

By the time they made it back to the palace, Merlin was feeling exhausted. Not only that but he was also perturbed by the strange looks Morgana had been giving him, and now, as the three of them stood in the council chamber, he wondered if she had seen him conjure up the wind. Was she about to give him away?

Suddenly the great doors swung open, and Uther entered the room. They bowed their heads respectfully as he swept across the chamber and took his position on the throne at the far end.

'You have some news for me, Arthur?' he said, his voice weary.

'Yes, Father,' said the prince, unable to suppress his smile any longer. 'Gaius and Merlin traced the source of the plague to the underground reservoir. I'm happy to report it's been destroyed.'

Uther stared at him incredulously. 'How?'

'It was a creature called an Afanc,' explained Arthur. 'We managed to corner it and kill it.'

He held out his hand and Merlin stepped forward and opened his bag. The prince fished out the blackened remains of one of the Afanc's claws and tossed it onto the palace floor.

Uther's lips parted in a smile, as if a great weight had been lifted from his shoulders. 'Can this really be true?' he breathed. 'The plague is at an end?'

'Yes, Father. And I therefore request that Gwen be released immediately.'

'So you've found the warlock then?'

Arthur looked round at the others. 'Well . . . not as yet . . .' he said uncertainly. 'There was no sign of anyone in the cavern.'

Uther's eyes narrowed. 'So you have no proof it wasn't the maidservant.'

Morgana stepped forward. 'This is ridiculous,' she said. 'Isn't it enough that the creature's dead? Even if Gwen was a witch, how could she have conjured such a thing when you have her bound in chains? She wasn't anywhere near the cavern!'

Uther met her gaze. 'I've warned you of her kind many times,' he said coldly. 'There is no one more cunning than a sorcerer. Who knows what deeds she was able to perform before she was captured?'

'Please, Father,' said Arthur, holding his arms out in appeal. 'At least grant a stay of execution now the disease is ended. I'm convinced the true sorcerer will reveal himself before long, and you will have all the proof you need.'

'You must listen to us,' begged Morgana desperately. 'Gwen is the innocent one in all this. She had nothing to do with summoning that creature!'

Uther said nothing as he considered their words. Merlin closed his eyes. What more could they do?

'Very well,' said the king at last. 'The execution is postponed for one day, but no more. If this sorcerer of yours doesn't show himself by tomorrow night, then the witch will burn as planned.'

Arthur's face fell. 'Yes, Father.' He bowed and the three of them left the room. As they walked along the corridor, the prince laid a hand on Merlin's shoulder. 'Are you all right?'

'Yes, I'm fine,' said Merlin quickly. 'I just need to be alone.'

He considered going to see Gwen, but then he remembered the promise he'd given her. It had to be about the most stupid thing he'd ever said. No way could he face her right now; at least she would find out from one of the others about her reprieve.

He realized there was nothing else for it, and he made his way back to Gaius' rooms. He found the physician had waited up for him, and he proceeded to fire all kinds of questions at him, keen to know about the Afanc and how it had been destroyed. But Merlin wasn't in the mood for celebrations. He made his excuses and sloped off to bed.

When he awoke the next morning, the sun was already high in the sky, light streaming through the window of his room. He washed and dressed hurriedly and ran into Gaius' room, just in time to see the old man coming through the main door, carrying a basketful of provisions.

'The news is out,' said Gaius happily. 'Just knowing the plague is over has lifted the mood of the whole city!'

Merlin shrugged and sat down at the table. 'That's good,' he said, but nothing was enough to lift his spirits. 'I've let Gwen down,' he said.

'You do know Arthur has rounded up every man available to look for the sorcerer?' said Gaius softly.

'They didn't find him before though, did they?' said Merlin, looking at him.

'That's true, but they're sure to turn up something this time.'

Merlin realized Gaius was doing his best to make him feel better. 'I suppose so,' he nodded.

Gaius paused. 'Are you sure you didn't see any sign of the sorcerer in the cavern?'

Merlin tried to think. 'No,' he said. 'We didn't see anyone at all . . . Oh, but hang on . . .' A thought struck him. 'There was just something . . .'

He jumped from his chair and darted up to his room, retrieving the piece of eggshell from his bag. 'I found this in the reservoir,' he said, running back down the stairs. 'I didn't think anything of it, but I knew it wasn't there when you and I looked.'

Gaius turned it over in his hand. 'Interesting . . .' he said.

'How come we missed it?'

'I don't know,' said Gaius. 'Perhaps it was brought to the surface when the creature burst out of the pool.' He reached for his glasses and perched them on the end of his nose, inspecting the shell more closely.

Merlin noticed a startled look pass over his face. 'What's the matter?'

'Merlin, are you really telling me you've had this since yesterday?' said Gaius, open-mouthed.

'Well, yes,' said Merlin. 'I just forgot all about it. Is it important?'

'Is it *important*?' Gaius repeated his words incredulously. 'Merlin, did it not even enter your head that this might be the very piece of evidence that we've been looking for?' He turned and made for the door. 'I have to see the king. I need to show him this immediately.'

'I'll come with you then.' Merlin went to grab his coat.

'No, you stay here out of harm's way,' said Gaius, holding up his hand. 'I fear when he sees this, he's not going to take the news well.'

Minutes later, Gaius entered the council chamber to find the king surrounded by a gathering of his most favoured nobles. He was downing a goblet of wine and was in a jovial mood, relieved at the recent turn of events.

'Good news, sire,' said Gaius. 'There are no new deaths and those who are sick are recovering.'

'Good!' exclaimed Uther, taking another swig of wine. 'It's strange – I've never even heard of an Afanc before . . .'

Hesitating, Gaius looked down, wishing there was

some other way of breaking the news. 'It's a creature conjured from clay by powerful magic. The type that can only be invoked by an ancient sorcerer. One who has the power to mirror the spirit of life . . .' His voice tailed off as the benign smile on the king's face vanished.

'What are you telling me?' whispered Uther.

Gaius reached into the pocket of his robe and produced the broken eggshell. 'This was found at the water source,' he said. 'It was part of an egg that must have contained the Afanc at the very start of its life.'

'Show me,' snapped Uther, taking the shell from Gaius.

'The mark it bears is unmistakable, sire,' said the physician softly. 'The mark of Nimueh.'

Uther looked and saw the rune Gaius was referring to – it looked like two adjoined letter Xs with a dot in the centre. 'No!' Uther blanched and turned away.

'We must be vigilant, sire,' said Gaius, grim-faced. 'She may have failed this time, but she will surely attempt to destroy Camelot again. She will not give up.'

Uther looked at him, his face ashen, appalled at the news and the terrible memories that had come back to haunt him. 'Will I never be rid of her . . .' he breathed, turning away. 'Nimueh . . .'

'Sire—'

'Leave me!' roared Uther. Shocked, the nobles turned and looked as he slumped himself down onto his throne, staring into space.

Realizing there was nothing else he could do, Gaius bowed graciously and went from the chamber, the nobles following hastily in his wake.

Uther sat on his throne in stony silence, a lonely figure in the huge room.

Chapter Eighteen

'I can't believe you didn't tell me!' said Merlin, shaking his head in disbelief.

'Eh? What was that?' Gaius was busy mixing a foul-looking potion and didn't even look up.

'About that eggshell,' said Merlin. 'I've been worrying about Gwen all this time and—'

There was a loud rap on the door and Merlin went to answer it. It was Arthur.

'I've spoken to Father,' he said, breaking into a smile. 'It took a while for him to calm down, but he's agreed to Gwen's immediate release.'

'I don't believe it!' Merlin gasped as a wave of euphoria swept over him. He really didn't know whether to laugh or cry.

'Everything all right, Merlin?' Arthur raised his eyebrows.

'Yes, yes,' laughed Merlin. 'I'm fine. Can I go and see her?'

'Yes, when you've tidied up my room,' said the prince.

Merlin's face fell. 'What?'

Arthur stood to one side and smirked. 'Go on,' he said. 'What are you waiting for?'

Merlin grinned and sped off, making for the dungeons. When he got there he found that Gwen had two visitors already – her father Tom, and Morgana, both waiting impatiently for the guard to release her. As the door to her cell swung open, Gwen leaped off her bench and threw herself into her father's arms, tears of joy rolling down her cheeks.

'I thought I was never going to see you again,' she cried, hugging him tightly, trying to blink away the tears. Then, letting him go for a moment, she turned to Merlin and Morgana. 'Thank you,' she said.

Morgana shook her head. 'Don't thank me,' she laughed. 'It was more Merlin.'

'Really?' Gwen glanced at him in surprise.

'Yes, he's the real hero here.'

'I don't know what to say,' she said softly.

'I didn't do anything,' Merlin said, shrugging off all the attention.

Gwen's father stepped forward and laid a protective arm on his daughter's shoulder. 'I'm grateful to you all,' he said. 'Come on, Gwen.'

She allowed herself to be led away, and as she left the cell, she flashed him a last smile of gratitude, and was gone.

Merlin was about to follow her from the dungeon, when Morgana called him back again.

'Merlin?' She was giving him a strange look. 'I just wanted you to know . . . your secret is safe with me.'

Merlin's heart leaped. 'My secret?' he said, trying to sound innocent.

'Come on, don't pretend. I know what you did.'

'You do?'

'I saw it with my own eyes.'

'You did?' Merlin was beginning to flap now. She must have caught sight of him using magic back in the tunnels.

'I understand why you don't want anyone to know,' said Morgana gently.

'Well . . . obviously . . .'

Her face broke out into a smile. 'I won't tell anyone.' Merlin sighed in relief, glad she wasn't about to go running to the king after all. 'You don't mind me talking to you about it, do you?'

'Oh no, it's . . .' Merlin stammered, amazed to find himself finally opening up to someone after all this time. 'You have no idea how hard it is to keep this hidden.'

'Well, you can continue to deny it, but . . . I think Gwen's a very lucky woman.'

Merlin blinked. '*Gwen?*'

Morgana held up a finger to her lips. 'It's all right, it's our secret.' She gave him a teasing smile and walked away, leaving Merlin alone in the cell.

Stunned, Merlin shook his head and chuckled, marvelling at how close he'd come to giving everything away. He left the dungeon in a daydream and wandered back to Gaius' room, turning over the events of the previous few days in his mind. Everything had worked out all right in the end. Surely he had nothing else to fear.

As he opened the door, he was astonished to find the dinner table all set out and Gaius himself busy stirring a big black pot which was bubbling away above the fire. The room was filled with delicious cooking smells.

'What's this?' asked Merlin. 'Are we expecting visitors or something?'

Gaius stopped stirring and looked up. 'Only you, Merlin. I thought I'd do you a fish stew to celebrate. Your favourite.'

Merlin beamed, realizing he hadn't really eaten properly for days. 'Thanks, that smells really good!' he said.

'Well, sit down then, it's ready,' said Gaius as he dished ladles of stew onto a plate and set it down on the table.

Ravenous, Merlin began tucking greedily into his food. He'd only taken a bite though when a thought hit him. 'Erm, this fish didn't come out of the water, did it?'

'Well, where else is it going to come from?' Gaius tutted.

Merlin grimaced and took another tentative mouthful.

'The water's fine now,' said Gaius. 'I've tested it myself, no sign of the disease at all.'

'All right, I believe you,' said Merlin. 'Anyway, I wanted to ask you more about that egg. So you know who it belonged to?'

'I'm afraid I do,' said Gaius solemnly. 'The plague was the work of a very powerful sorceress. Her name is Nimueh – and she is an ancient enemy of Uther's. I just hope for your sake you haven't come to her attention.'

'Doubt it,' said Merlin, making a face.

Gaius raised an eyebrow.

'Well, no one else seems to appreciate my skills,' carried on Merlin. 'I just want someone to see me for who I am.'

Gaius poured him some more wine. 'One day, Merlin, one day . . . '

'One day what?'

'One day people won't believe what an *idiot* you were.'

'Thanks,' said Merlin. He watched the old physician as his rumpled features broke into a grin. He suddenly looked twenty years younger.

Gaius held up his goblet and clanked it against Merlin's, and they each took a generous swig.

Far away in the chamber of ice, a rippling image appeared on the surface of the restless, swirling waters. The woman – Nimueh – gave a sneer of contempt as she observed the old fool Gaius and his boy sorcerer enjoying their feast.

She contemplated his wide, innocent eyes, remembering the power she'd witnessed in the cavern – the magic that had destroyed her precious creature and brought her plans to nothing.

It was a deed that couldn't go unpunished.

She lashed out at the pool in anger and the waters hissed and bubbled, the image dissolving into fragments.

'We shall meet again,' she breathed. 'Merlin, you will pay for this.'

COMING SOON

The Poisoned Chalice

Text by Simon Forward

Based on the story by Ben Vanstone

BANTAM BOOKS

Chapter One

Preparation was key. The devil was in the detail, so it was said. And just as a story had to be told with feeling, just as a song had to be sung from the heart, so the true power of a spell lay in more than the incantations and material ingredients.

So Nimueh held onto the tiny stab of pain in her finger, where she had pricked it with a needle, for some measure of that sting would be going into the magic along with her blood. There was venom in her words as she sent them echoing around her cavern.

'*We Gar-Dena in geardagum . . .*'

The shadows, her only audience, would play their part too. And the stalactites of glassy silica, like daggers of ice stabbing down over the scene.

'*. . . theodcyninga thrym gefrunon . . .*'

She held her finger over the basin, pointing downwards like the stalactites, and allowed the blood to drip into the water. The droplets broke apart on the surface and sank slowly, creating red swirls.

'. . . *hu tha aethelingas ellen fremedon!*'

As she stepped up the speed of the incantation, she dipped her hand into the bowl and stirred the contents with her fingers, whipping the blood into crimson clouds.

'*Sythan aerest wearth feasceaft funden.*' Faster and louder she poured the words forth. '*Hyran scolde thara, ofer hronrade Camelot, hyran scolde.*'

There! A glimmer of light rippled across the surface of the bloody whirlpool.

'Merlin!' She hurled the name at the shadows, soaking up the sound as it bounced back at her. Yes, there was power in the name, amplified in those echoes; power that would do him no good against her.

The light in the water dappled and the spots of colour resolved themselves into an image. Clear as a mirror. Sharper, even. Her window into Camelot was open and in it she could see him: Merlin. The servant, polishing chain mail for his master. A smile pasted onto his face, despite his dull labours.

Nimueh's face twisted into a smile too, but hers was

nothing like Merlin's. Hers was edged like a knife blade. A cruel celebration, laughing silently at this servant. Small wonder that it was so easy to summon his image in the scrying bowl. Servants were easily summoned. They were a property, after all, to be utilized or disposed of as their masters saw fit. *Well, Merlin,* she thought, still smiling, *I am the master of you.*

Time to proceed.

'*Hyran scolde thara, ofer hronrade Camelot, hyran scolde Merlin.*'

Delicately, between two fingers, she picked up the flower that lay on the rim of the basin. Her pricked finger enriched the yellow of the petals with a faint bloodstain. The minutest drop of her own life, to reinforce the death bound up in the spell. The devil truly *was* in the detail.

Nimueh plucked the single stained petal and dropped it into the water. It floated on the surface like the frailest of boats.

She watched its aimless voyage for thirteen heartbeats. Then she dipped her fingers into the water and scooped it up. The colours had drained away to nothing, leaving only a fragile petal, translucent as a fly's wing.

With her other hand she reached for the goblet that

lay waiting on a velvet cloth. Gleaming gold, its base was embellished with a finely crafted floral design studded with rubies. Nimueh would have preferred emeralds to mirror her own eyes. But of course this goblet had to be a perfect match for the one it was intended to replace.

Lovingly she pressed the enchanted petal into the cup. There it stayed, adhering to the metal and well camouflaged against the gold. Gold, like a pretty girl, had the power to dazzle; when presented with such treasures, men were often blind to anything else.

Nimueh set the goblet down on its cloth.

Preparation was key; her preparations were done.

Time to deliver her gift.

There might have been a war on, the way Gaius came rushing into Merlin's room, urging him to get himself out of bed. Even worse, when he emerged from his room, pulling on his jacket, Gaius hit him with the news that there was 'No time for breakfast'.

Merlin chased after Gaius, keen to make sure the old man heard his grumbling stomach – and for answers as to what on earth was going on. Since questions were all he was going to be full of this morning, it seemed only fair that he should be supplied with a few explanations.

As far as he knew, it was supposed to be a normal day of servitude, acting as general gopher and dogsbody for Arthur.

'Bayard is coming,' Gaius informed him. Which was a little too cryptic to satisfy Merlin's appetite. 'Uther wants to ensure he is met with a large enough reception committee. And that includes servants and court physicians.'

'So who is this Bayard?'

'Look there.'

Merlin had been vaguely conscious that Gaius was straying from their usual route to the palace; now the old man halted by a window and pointed over the rooftops and battlements. Merlin peered out beyond the city walls.

The road into Camelot had become a river of blue, thundering uphill to the gates. Not literally, of course. Although a magical transformation on that scale would certainly have explained the urgency. No, this was a flood of men on horseback, decked out in tabards and cloaks of an almost heavenly blue. Trailing after them came a long string of wagons, and flocks of attendants and servants following along on foot.

'The Knights of Mercia,' said Gaius, gesturing at the impressive sight with a nod. 'It has been many a year since so many were seen so close to Camelot's walls. In the past,' he added gravely, 'their presence alone would have been an act of war.'

Merlin took in the numbers of troops and the supporting wagons. It looked like an army to him. 'And what is it today?'

'Peace, Merlin. An act of peace. Or at least, we hope, a beginning.'

Gaius hastened on his way down the passage, an invitation to Merlin to follow.

'Hence all the fuss about numbers at the reception,' the old man went on. 'This kind of occasion can stand or fall on the details.'

Merlin realized that Arthur must have known about this, could have told him; probably *should* have told him. But Arthur did love to spring these big, important events on him at the last minute and have him come running. Having servants running about was apparently part of the natural order of things.

Merlin wondered what they could possibly want him for. He hoped that they only needed him to stand there and look – he glanced down at his hastily thrown-on clothes – passably smart. He was intrigued and excited, eager to know more about what the event entailed. He had never attended a peace conference before.

Hurrying after Gaius, he prayed that his stomach wouldn't rumble at too crucial a moment.

It was a grand occasion, the blue of Mercia sweeping into the throne room to clash with the red of Camelot. King Uther stood before the throne, flanked by his son, members of the royal court and his knights; these in turn backed up by a small legion of maids and servants. Bayard stopped a short distance in front of the king, his entire entourage coming to a halt on cue behind him.

Tension fixed the tableau in place. The colours warred silently with each other. Two armies faced each other on what, for all its polished boards and hanging tapestries, could have been a battlefield. Condensed and concentrated in this chamber was all the enmity and spilled blood between these two nations, these two forces, these two men.

That in itself was a power to rival magic.

Uther spoke first. 'Camelot welcomes you, Bayard of Mercia.' There was frost in his voice, betraying the superficial warmth of the words.

Bayard was a tall figure, his features as stern and weathered as Uther's, but rather more grizzled, his long reddish hair and dark beard salted with plenty of grey.

He answered with some ice of his own. 'And what about you?'

'You killed a lot of my men, many of them friends,' Uther replied.

This was about more than history and armies. This was personal.

'As were the soldiers I lost,' retorted Bayard.

Peace might have ended right there and then. Instead, Uther steeled himself and held out his hand, almost defying his guest to refuse it.

'Which is why the fighting has to stop,' he declared. 'The treaty we sign today marks an end to the war and the beginning of a new friendship between our people.'

Bayard took a pace forward and reached for Uther's hand. Although at this stage it amounted to no more than words and gestures, the rites had to be observed if peace were to have any chance of success.

Much like a spell, in that respect. The incantations, the ingredients, the setting – and the emotion – invested in this moment; they all played their part.

Through all this, Merlin stood discreetly behind his master, the young Prince Arthur, his head bowed to hide the remnants of sleep still in his eyes.

Nimueh, from her own position among the ranks of

Bayard's servants, enjoyed his efforts to look meek and humble. Quite the actor. None of the intricacies or import of the ceremony being played out were lost on her, but they were ultimately of only passing interest. Most of her attention was focused on Merlin.

She was looking forward to making his acquaintance.

A servant – she smiled to herself – to be used and disposed of as she saw fit.

Chapter Two

Once the formal meet and greet was over, the two parties broke up and went their separate ways. Meanwhile Merlin overheard – with dismay – that Uther and Bayard would be breakfasting together. Breakfasting!

But he had to suppress his groan as Arthur took him aside for a quiet talk. 'Merlin. We need you to help unload Bayard's wagons, install their things in their quarters. We need you to be our spy in their camp.'

'Are you serious?' quizzed Merlin.

Arthur's face betrayed nothing. 'Of course. Don't worry – nobody would look twice at you. They'd never suspect.'

For a second Merlin almost believed it – that was all Arthur wanted. Then he laughed and rolled his eyes. 'In other words you just want me to lug stuff from the wagons to their rooms.'

'Pretty much.' Arthur grinned. 'Good luck with your mission.'

He swaggered off, probably to sit down to a slap-up breakfast with his father and their guest. Merlin would have loved to give him a slap-up something.

Apparently servants were something to be freely passed around between masters, handed out on loan. He guessed it lent a touch of variety to the job: you got to cart stuff around for different people.

His stomach still asking for permission to grumble, Merlin headed off on his 'mission'.

No more than half an hour later, he was joining the long stream of servants trudging back and forth between the wagons in the courtyard and the chambers that had been assigned to the Mercian guests. He couldn't believe how much stuff they had to offload – he sincerely hoped it was all going to be left as part of some peace offering when they departed. As olive branches went, it was all a bit ordinary: among the sundry supplies and effects, they had even brought their own bedding, as though Camelot linen wasn't good enough. Although, to be fair, many of the chambers allocated to the Mercians had never served as bedrooms. Because Camelot was unaccustomed to catering for quite so many guests at the same time, the arrangements were all very makeshift; although he gathered that – fairly naturally – Lord Bayard himself had been granted one of the finest rooms.

Not that Merlin would ever see it. He had been told that it was locked and that only the most trusted of the Mercian staff would be permitted to enter.

No, the goods he was hauling around were intended only for the lower orders of the Mercian entourage. That figured: Merlin was probably serving the servants.

Oh well, count your blessings, as his mother always told him. At least it was a sunny day. Daylight poured in between the columns as he plodded along the cloistered passage to the 'guest wing', weighed down by two sacks of . . . something.

'What's in here?' he had asked the guard who tossed them down from the wagon. Whatever it was, each sack had nearly knocked him flat as he did his best to catch it.

'None of your beeswax,' growled the guard. 'And don't you go poking your nose in.'

Merlin had no suspicions that the contents were anything sinister. He simply wondered why the Mercians couldn't have travelled light. Peace was a long-winded process, apparently, and they were planning on staying a while.

The sacks didn't clank or make any noise, but they were bulky and awkward to carry. And they made his arms ache after only a few yards.

Merlin saw Gaius strolling along the passage. Empty-handed, of course. The court physician was exempt from such heavy labours.

'Why do I always get landed with the donkey work?' Merlin complained. Actually, he didn't really mind and was happy to be involved, but the opportunity to win some sympathy from Gaius was too good to pass up.

Gaius smiled. 'You're a servant, Merlin; it's what you do.'

Gaius was a kindly old man, but that never stopped him extracting a good deal of amusement from Merlin's position as Arthur's dogsbody.

'My arms will be a foot longer by the time I get this lot inside.' Merlin took advantage of the fact that Gaius had paused to chat and lowered the sacks to the ground for a welcome break. Other servants continued to file past with their own burdens.

'It's character-building,' the old man assured him. 'As the old proverb says – hard work breeds' – Gaius' memory appeared to have failed him momentarily – 'a harder soul.'

Merlin gave the physician a sidelong look. 'There's no way that's a proverb. You just made that up.'

'No I didn't,' Gaius lied. Badly.

Passing between them just then, a girl stumbled in front of Merlin. She dropped onto one knee, her bundle of cushions and neatly folded bedlinen strewn in disarray across the flagstones.

'Sorry . . . excuse me.' She blushed coyly and reached across to gather up the items.

'It's all right. Let me give you a hand with that,' volunteered Merlin.

He crouched down to help her pick up her things and was conscious of their sudden closeness. Immediately he realized he was looking down the front of her dress. Feeling a rush of embarrassment warming his cheeks, he quickly aimed his gaze higher and locked onto her face.

She was pretty. Stunning, in fact. Pretty stunning.

Emerald-green eyes sparkled against a beautifully milky complexion. Strands of gorgeous dark hair dangled fetchingly loose from under a blue turban. Smooth shoulders were, tantalizingly bare above a simple dress of rich burgundy and Mercian blue.

She finished restoring her burden to a reasonably tidy pile while Merlin retrieved the last of the items: a red velvet cushion.

They rose together, Merlin's eyes still fixed on her. He couldn't help himself.

'Hi,' he ventured. 'I'm Merlin.' He proffered his hand.

She took it in soft, slender fingers; gave it a delicate shake. Her touch was cool and precious, and Merlin fancied he could still feel its light pressure after she'd let go of his hand.

'Kara,' she said in a sweetly shy voice. 'You're Arthur's servant. That must be such an honour.'

An honour? Yes. Bless her, she didn't need to hear the real story of life in Arthur's service. It was Merlin's turn to lie. He resolved to do a better job than Gaius. 'Oh yeah, it is. Well – someone's got to keep the place running.'

For the first time in what seemed like ages, he was aware of Gaius still standing there. The old man was looking at him over Kara's shoulder, arching a wry eyebrow.

Merlin's friendly banter stalled in self-conscious silence.

'Thank you, Merlin,' said Kara. And she glanced down at his hands.

'Hmm?' said Merlin. He noticed that he was still holding the cushion and realized she was probably hoping he might return it at some point. 'Oh, right. Yeah – no problem.'

He handed it back, stacking it on top of her pile. Then he looked at her, stuck for anything more to say. Actually, he was full of things he could say, but he was sure that if he attempted to speak them out loud, they would tumble out in an incoherent stream that would only make him sound stupid. As a safer alternative, his lips sealed themselves into a smile.

Kara returned it, sugaring her smile with a flash of her bright eyes. Merlin was captivated by their sparkle.

Too soon, she bobbed in a little curtsy – 'It was nice meeting you' – then went gracefully on her way.

Merlin turned and allowed his gaze to linger on her receding figure.

'Shouldn't you be busy "running the place".' Gaius' dry tones summoned Merlin back to the present.

He laughed and shrugged. He had to allow the old man his joke. He fended it off with a smile, and might even have joined in the laughter if it hadn't been for the sight of the two sacks waiting at his feet.

Sighing, he hoisted them up again, feeling that his

accidental meeting with the girl had lightened his load, even if only a little.

Nimueh savoured the delights of her recent encounter. To Merlin, it would have seemed so natural, so accidental. For her, it was merely one more essential step in her preparations. It had gone precisely according to plan. No, better than anticipated.

There had never been any question in her mind that he would prove susceptible to her charms. But of course it was always difficult to predict just how susceptible.

Oh yes, when she next spoke to him, his rapt attention was assured. She would be able to play him like a musical instrument.

She stopped and tucked herself out of sight. A guard passed by down the corridor without so much as turning his head.

Nimueh knew when to be noticed and when it was better not to be seen. It wouldn't have been disastrous to be spotted: she could have offered up any number of convincing reasons for her presence here in a passage so near to Bayard's chamber. But it was as well to avoid arousing even passing suspicions at this stage.

Watching as the guard disappeared round the corner,

she continued along the corridor, climbing a short flight of steps and coming to a halt outside a large wooden door. The carving and the finish of the wood told her all she needed to know about the importance of the room.

She waved a hand over the lock and whispered: '*Alysan duru ronne.*'

The tumblers turned over with an iron clunk.

Nimueh opened the door and slipped inside.

She swiftly scanned the room. A grand four-poster bed, a few chairs and side tables, along with shields and hangings boasting the white castle crest of Mercia to help the guest feel at home. But she wasn't interested in the furnishings or the decor.

There.

An oak box rested on the bedside table. It too was draped with a sash bearing the Mercian castle emblem. Nimueh flipped back the sash and lifted the lid. The interior was lined with rich blue silk. The perfect setting for the two golden goblets she knew she would find inside.

Far from being a pair, the two were quite different from one another. The only one she was concerned with had a base fashioned in a familiar floral design, set with rubies. Satisfied that her scrying abilities had not let her down, Nimueh unpacked the small cloth parcel that had been the one item in her bundle she had taken care not to drop. Setting it on the table, she unwrapped it to unveil her own goblet, lying attractively on its velvet cloth.

Removing its twin from the box, she picked up her forgery and laid it inside. The original she laid on the velvet cloth and wrapped up, ready to be taken away.

She closed the box and replaced the drape exactly as she had found it, with the care and precision of a huntress setting a trap.

A smile played across her lips as she thought of her unsuspecting prey.

ALSO AVAILABLE

THE DRAGON'S CALL

When Merlin arrives in the great kingdom of Camelot he discovers a dark side to the bustling city: magic is outlawed on pain of death! If he wants to stay alive, Merlin will have to keep his unique magical talents a closely guarded secret . . .

978 0 553 82109 3

ALSO AVAILABLE

VALIANT

A mysterious new knight arrives in Camelot for the sword tournament. His fighting skills are impressive but when an opponent is not just injured but *poisoned*, Merlin suspects that dark magic is involved. Merlin is determined to expose the evil, but Arthur is next in line to fight and time is running out . . .

978 0 553 82110 9

ALSO AVAILABLE

MERLIN MYSTERY ACTIVITY BOOK

A mysterious stranger has taken Arthur prisoner and Merlin has to find him and set him free. Join Merlin on a dangerous journey to save Arthur. Work through the puzzles, play the games and answer the riddles to help Merlin save his friend, the future king of Camelot.

This activity book includes a free spell notebook!

978 0 553 82105 5

ALSO AVAILABLE

MERLIN QUEST ACTIVITY BOOK

This Quest Activity book sets the stage
for tournament day in Camelot. But
danger lurks around every corner. An evil
knight threatens Arthur, can he defeat him
in battle? Join Arthur and his friends on
their adventure around Camelot. Solve the
puzzles, play the games and answer the
riddles to help Arthur defeat the evil
knight and win the tournament.

This activity book includes a
free pull-out game!

978 0 553 82106 2

ALSO AVAILABLE
FOR YOUNGER READERS

THE MAGIC BEGINS

Merlin arrives in Camelot full of excitement
and eager for adventure. But sorcery is
outlawed here and so he must learn
to hide his own magical talents.

When a mysterious new knight turns up
for the sword tournament, Merlin suspects
that dark magic is involved. He's determined
to investigate, but soon finds that keeping the
magic secret – and Prince Arthur alive –
is much harder than he thought . . .

978 0 553 82111 6

ALSO AVAILABLE

A FIGHTING CHANCE

Merlin wants to help his new friend,
Lancelot, become a Knight of Camelot
– but it's not as easy as he hopes.

Then the Lady Morgana is struck down
by a mystery illness. Gaius is baffled and a
new physician arrives to help. He seems to
have all the answers, but Merlin suspects that
there's something sinister going on.

978 0 553 82501 5

ALSO AVAILABLE

SWORD AND SORCERY

When Merlin and Morgana join forces to save a child the king has commanded be put to death, they soon discover that going against King Uther could prove fatal.

Meanwhile, a mysterious black knight arrives to challenge the Knights of Camelot to mortal combat. Old secrets, long hidden, are stirring and the king is afraid for his only son. The black knight seems invincible and Merlin senses that only magic can stop him . . .

978 0 553 82502 2